This Book belongs to:

James McDONALD

JOHNNY CASANOVA

Books by the same author

Ghostly Tales for Ghastly Kids

Grizzly Tales for Gruesome Kids

The Dreaded Lurgie

JOHNNY CASANOVA

The Unstoppable Sex Machine

JAMIE RIX

WALKER BOOKS
AND SUBSIDIARIES
LONDON • BOSTON • SYDNEY

To the girl in the purple uniform
(Whoever you are)

First published 1996 by Walker Books Ltd
87 Vauxhall Walk, London SE11 5HJ

Text © 1996 Jamie Rix
Cover illustration © 1996 Nick Sharratt

2 4 6 8 10 9 7 5 3 1

This book has been typeset in Sabon.

Printed in England

British Library Cataloguing in Publication Data
A catalogue record for this book is available
from the British Library.

ISBN 0-7445-2498-9

CONTENTS

1
THE UNSTOPPABLE SEX MACHINE

"The name's Worms. Johnny Worms. They call me the unstoppable sex machine, 'cause I'm hot to trot. I'm a red hot chilli pepper with cayenne sauce. I'm a townie tiger with a rrrrrrapacious appetite. And when the ladies set their eyes on me I'm the London Fire Brigade's worst nightmare! I'm talking lickin' chickens, you understand, flaming feminines, 'cause when I set their hearts on fire there ain't no river wet enough to put 'em out!" I flicked the fringe out of my eyebrows and pouted into the bathroom mirror. I loved the thought that nobody else could see me standing on top of the loo seat using a toothpaste tube as a microphone. I wiggled my powerful hips inside my Mickey Mouse boxer shorts, thrust up my arms in a dashing, ride-'em-cowboy sort of a pose and blew myself a well deserved kiss. "My God, but you're handsome!" I said to my own reflection. "How could Alison possibly resist? She'll faint when you ask her to marry you." There was a loud knock at the door, which made me jump.

"I with you'd huwwy up in there," lisped my baby sister in that weary tone of voice she'd copied off Mum. "If Teddy doethn't go to the toilet thoon, he'th going to have a vewy nathty accident all over Mummy'th carpet."

"Go and get the carpet shampoo," I said. "I haven't done my hair yet."

"But you've been in there for wover a nour!" she moaned. It was time to give Sherene a lesson in Major Life Priorities. I took my tub of gel off the sink and bent down by the keyhole.

"Listen, little sister, I'll let you into a secret..." I wanted her to think that I was going to reveal something really, really important, something she was far too young to know, because then she was guaranteed to do exactly what I said in order to hear it. "Put your ear as close to the door as you can." Sherene pressed herself up against the plywood panel. I could see the pinkness of her ear through the keyhole.

"Well, go on then," she urged, impatiently, "impreth me." Well, she did ask. I took a scoop of blue hair gel out of the pot and impressed it right through the keyhole until it squirted out the other end and filled up her lughole to overflowing, like one of those cake-shop doughnuts with plastic cream in the middle. It was totally scam-cessful, but Sherene failed to see the funny side. She just bawled.

"MUMMY! Johnny'th gone and put the jelly in my earholeth!" and she ran off to exaggerate the story to Mum, so that she could have the pleasure of watching me getting duffed up.

"Huh, kids!" I snarled, curling my top lip like Bruce Willis in I'm-harder-than-a-hard-hat, no-tears, muscle-man mode.

The gel pot was now half empty, but there was still enough for me to perform the solemn ceremony of the Preparation of the Sacred Hair. I filled the basin with lukewarm water and plunged my head in up to the neck. The water worked miracles on the ridges, valleys, lumps, bumps and sticking-up cows' licks that last night's pillow had creased into my hair, flattening them on to my scalp like a swimming cap. I half-dried it with a towel and brushed the tangles out with my dad's comb, scraping the dark wet strands behind my ears until I looked like one of those gigolo blokes from that ballroom-dancing programme, the ones with the tight trousers. Dead Spanish Matador, I thought, imagining a rose between my teeth and a bull at my heels. The crowd roared. The bull's horns were inches away

9

from my perfectly rounded bottom. The women were standing all around the bull ring, handkerchiefs stuffed into their mouths, tears rolling down their cheeks, begging the bull not to gore me! A million and one people held their breath. Cars stopped on motorways to listen on their radios. Boats sank, aeroplanes crashed, even God stopped creating for a bit ... and then, with one lightning swivel of my elastic hips, I turned and faced the ton of charging topside, dispatching it swiftly between its shoulder blades with a single lunge from dad's electric toothbrush.

"Hurry up in there, Johnny, will you? Some of us have got gnomes to feed before going to work, you know." Talk of the devil, there he was, regular as clockwork. My dad. Every morning at 7.15 he'd say exactly the same thing, and every morning I never finished doing my hair before 7.25, so I don't know why he bothered. I still had my topknot to titivate. It was time for the gelling. The artistic engine room of hair styling. With water you can iron out any overnight horrors (like Hair Horns or Falling Fringes), but with gel you can create a thing of genuine beauty, a classic work of art that would sell for millions if you peeled your scalp off the top of your head and mounted it in a display case. Gel, in my opinion, is what girls most like about boys. That and money. So I rubbed a clear blue fistful of the stuff into my locks until they were stiff and sticky like papier mâché. Then I spread the gunge evenly across my scalp with a cake mix scraper that I'd nicked out of the kitchen, and shaped, fussed and patted till my head looked like a speed cyclist's helmet. Solid Darth Vader. Black, shiny and hard as a coal scuttle. Not a hair moved, not even when I turned my head upside down to study my immaculate styling through my legs. It was 7.25. I was ready to face the world.

When I opened the door, my dad was outside tapping his foot on the carpet. He had his shaving towel draped over his arm like a waiter and his breath smelt sour. He always wore the same thing. A red, shiny dressing gown (with a gold T for Terry on both lapels), red leather slippers (with the heel trodden down) and light blue pyjamas, buttoned right up to the top, to stop Mum getting her hands on him. He's a reedy man, a bit thin and scraggy round the edges, the sort you can see through if you shine a torch on his chest, at least that's what my mate Ginger said, but I've never tried it. My biggest worry is that one day I'll grow up to be like him. Bulging veins, spindly wrists, all teeth and glasses. Little, black, round-framed glasses which sit neatly on the bridge of his nose, come rain, shine, bath or swim. He says he can't see without them, but it doesn't hurt to try occasionally, does it, especially when you're out in public and you don't want your mates to think your dad's a weedy gink? He's a creature of habit: same newspaper, same breakfast, same house, same bus, same job, same lunch, same gin and tonic, same bedtime and same chapter in the same book for twenty years. The man's a walking museum, and he sings Elvis Presley hits in the bath which is even more embarrassing, because he doesn't look one bit like Elvis, and maybe everyone thinks that he thinks that he does, or maybe everyone thinks that I keep telling him that he does, which is even worse, because I wouldn't be that stupid! But there again, maybe they think I am that stupid, that's my point. Anyway, on this particular day, as every day, my mega-boring dad was standing outside the bathroom as I came out.

"Morning, son," he said, ruffling my hair, like he was patting a dog for fetching a stick. "Having fun?"

Was I having fun? Let's examine the situation. I had just spent the best part of an hour getting my crowning glory done up perfect for school (and Alison), then he comes along and collapses it! Was I having fun? Was I hell. My exquisitely crafted hair sculpture had just tumbled over my eyes, like a poorly pasted sheet of wallpaper!

* * *

12

"Ooooooo-hoooooo!" The Worms' mating call rang through the house like a burst of Tarzan's jungle-yodelling. My Mum was calling her family to table.

She whacked the back of my knees with a fish slice as I walked into the kitchen.

"Mornin', ducks," she said. "That's for teasing Sherene. Now, scrambled, fried, poached, boiled or just raw with a dash of brown sauce?" She was cooking eggs for breakfast.

"Nothing," I said, lowering myself gingerly into my seat so as not to ruin the crease in my school trousers. "I'm on a diet."

"Well, excuse me," snorted Mum. "You're on a what?"

"Mummy," interrupted Sherene, "I think the doggie'th jutht done a thmelly woopth." The dog was a bloodhound called Pongo, with Very Leaky Bowel Syndrome, which meant that he smelled disgusting, especially when his lower intestine vaporized over the breakfast table.

"Can't we put a cork up there or something?" I suggested, but Mum threw her arms protectively around Pongo's neck.

"No, we can't!" she quivered. "I wouldn't do that to you, would I? And Pongo's just as much a part of our little family. Now don't get me wrong, I find his little smells at table just as nasty as you do, but he's so sweet, isn't he? Look at those lovely, big, saggy eyes trying to say he's sorry." Actually those lovely, big, saggy eyes were trying to say that a second smell would shortly be joining us for break-fast, and perhaps we'd all like to leave the kitchen, but a bloodhound's eyes always look like they're apologizing for something or other and Mum hasn't twigged that yet. The table cloth fluttered gently as Pongo fulfilled his promise, while Mum turned the conversation back to diets. "What's a boy your age need to slim for? You're all skin and bone."

"My physique is the talking point of the shower room," I replied, indignantly. "I bet Arnold Schwarzenegger's mum doesn't force him to eat eggs in the morning." At the men-tion of Arnie, Mum's eyes glazed over and a thin tendril of dribble drooled over her bottom lip. I knew the look. She was dreaming of firm flesh and hairy biceps. "Your Uncle Stan looked like that once, you know, before all his muscles slipped down to his stomach. He's nice, isn't he, Stan? Cuddly."

"No. He'th fat and ugly," said Sherene, "and breatheth beer." Then she trilled, mis-cheviously, "I'll tell you why Johnny'th on a diet."

"You dare!" I said, realizing she'd over-heard what I'd said in the bathroom.

"He'th going to propothe marriage to Alithon today, that'th why!"

"Shut up, Sherene. I'm not!" I shouted,

storming from the table in a hair-tossing huff, but my sneaky, snitchy sister had got it in one. I adored Alison Mallinson. I swooned at the mere mention of her name. She was drop-dead gorgeous, the most desirable creature that ever wore a grey pleated skirt and knee-length socks, and although she didn't know it she was going to be my pinny-pink princess, my pash, my paramour, my powder-puff partner till the end of time! All of this I don't mind admitting to the bathroom mirror, but it's not something you want your mum telling the neighbours, is it?

ON PONGO AND LUV

Luv unlike a doggy smell,
Which follows you and makes life hell,
Is really quite a luvly thing,
It makes you want to talk and sing.
The other thing on which to touch
Is why girls luv me so very much.
I think it's 'cause I make them laugh
And do ten press-ups in the bath.
(Every day, I'll have you know.)

(Johnny Worms, Aged 13 — From
his unpublished collection of poems,
"LUV TICKLES A BIT")

2
THE APPLE OF MY EYE

What my best mate Ginger and I like to do best when we hide out in the school loos is to make the first years pee on the seat. We wait until they're past the point of no return, when even a plumber with a monkey wrench can't turn you off, and then leap up, put our faces over the top of the cubicle door and shout, "Smile, you're on Candid Camera!" If we get lucky they turn round and splash their shoes as well as the seat, which is worth two extra points. Ginger's just flukey, I think, because there's no difference in our techniques, but he's got masses more points than me. He says it's because he can shout louder, on account of him having bigger lungs and I've got little lover's lungs, which are only good for whispering sweet nothings.

So, that morning, Ginger and I had sneaked

into the loos before assembly, and Ginger wanted to play the "seat-wetting" game, but I told him I had more important things to do with my time.

"Like what?" he said, disbelievingly.

"Promise not to tell?" I asked, locking the cubicle door. He crossed himself all over.

"On pain of death and you can have my twelve-inch pencil case if I do." That was good enough for me. Everyone wanted Ginger's pencil case, because he could get a full size ruler in it.

"OK, you're on," I said to him. "Well, last night I went to bed a boy and this morning I woke up a man!"

"What man?" said Ginger. "Your dad?"

"No! I ... ME ... JOHNNY WORMS ... I woke up with manly feelings!"

"You've grown a hair in your armpit, haven't you?" grunted Ginger, full of repressed jealousy.

"I'm not talking about hairy armpits," I said. "I'm talking about emotions, Ginger. I'm in love." Ginger laughed.

"With yourself," he snorted.

"With Alison Mallinson," I replied, sharply. I paused to let the wonderful news sink in, but Ginger already knew what he thought. He didn't like it. Actually, it was Alison he didn't like, or, to be more accurate, girls in general. They weren't good enough at football for

Ginger. Not to mention the fact that they cried non-stop, stole his best friend (that's me) and, when he did spend time with them, either stopped him from doing what he liked best (which was football) or tidied him up. He couldn't see the point in making friends with someone who didn't like him the way he was. He was a scruff-bucket. "A lump of sheep's offal tied round the middle with string" was what his mum called him. It was fair enough really, because his shirt was always flapping, his socks never matched, his blazer was more patch than blazer, his shoes were scuffed white and he had this horrible habit of picking his nose and wiping the bits on the back of his tie.

"Boring," he said. "I thought you were going to tell me you'd met Ryan Giggs or something." I told my *ex*-best friend Ginger I'd be grateful if he could stop thinking about himself for a moment and start thinking about me instead.

"Do you think it's easy being in love?" I said. Ginger shrugged and picked a scab on the back of his hand.

"Dunno," he replied.

"It makes you do really stupid things that you wouldn't normally do."

"Like dump on your friends," he muttered, bitterly.

"No. Like cycle in the rain and buy each other chips, that sort of thing. But, and here's the difficult bit, girls want you to keep saying "I love you, darling," and things like that, all the time. And you try making "I love you, darling," sound different every time. It's hard. Actually, it's harder making it sound like you mean it, but that's why I need your help, Ginger. I've got to win Alison's heart and I don't know what to say."

"Your prayers?" smiled Ginger, helpfully. "If Timothy Winchester ever gets to hear about this, he'll kill you."

"Timothy Winchester!" I sneered. "Huh! That puffed-up windbag doesn't scare me. I could duff him up with one foot tied behind my back."

"No, you couldn't."

"I could."

"Couldn't."

"Could."

"Couldn't."

"Could."

"Couldn't." We're good conversationalists, Ginger and I.

"How do you know?"

"Because Timothy Winchester can break a ruler between his knees and Cecil said he saw him nut a desk and leave a huge dent in it."

"Yeah, in his head," I said.

"In the desk," said Ginger. "Plus, he's told everyone he's going to marry Alison when he's got a mortgage. I wouldn't mess with him."

"Bet he hasn't told Alison," I said, pretending not to care, "and I know for a fact that she wouldn't have him, because his arms are too long, like a monkey's."

"He's got money," said Ginger.

"Will you shut up!" I shouted. "You're supposed to be supporting me." Ginger stood up.

"You're mad," he said. "I'm going outside for a game of football. If you've got any sense you'll forget about Alison and come with me."

"Love knows not what is sense," I said profoundly.

"Then love's a plonker," said Ginger. "Have a nice beating-up." And he left.

A FLEETING GLANCE AT LUV
AND HATE

Luv
Hurts
(Or so they say),
But
Hate
Hurts more
When it hits you.

(Johnny Worms — In pain on the pan)

I took out a set of coloured pencils and a

piece of card and laid them out on top of the cistern. I had decided to melt Alison's heart with a personalized love postcard. This was like a letter only shorter and more direct, like taking a girl to the cinema and getting straight into the snogging by the sweet counter in the foyer. I started off by drawing a huge red heart in the top left hand corner. It wasn't quite as symmetrical as I had hoped, in fact it leaned over alarmingly to one side, like it was made of ice cream and left too close to the fire. Actually, it didn't look like a heart at all, more like a rotten apple. So I added in a couple of green leaves and a stalk and wrote underneath:

You is the apple of my eye.
Cor! I bet you taste good with custard!

That was good. She'd probably laugh at that. Now for the important bit. I sat back on the toilet seat, sucked on my pencil and let the muse take me.

Alison, Alison,
When can I see you some?
My heart is all cooked and done,
For a blinder called Alison
(Mallinson).

luv
JW

I added in the Mallinson just in case she thought I was talking about a different Alison, and then I put it in brackets just in case using her surname was too formal and offended her (after all, it was a bit of a bank-managerish thing to do). Anyway, I was pretty confident that the note would move her to tears. I turned the card over and drew a huge pair of lips on the front. Underneath, I wrote the letters S. W. A. L. K., and then added some seagulls, because I'm good at drawing them. I can draw hills and car wheels too (if the rest of the car is out of the picture), but I thought, on balance, that seagulls were more romantic and symbolic of my soaring passion. As a final gesture of serious desire, I kissed the love postcard and imagined it was Alison.

When I opened my eyes, I swear I saw the ghost of William Shakespeare hanging off the hook on the back of the loo door. He was penning a love sonnet with his right hand and giving me the big thumbs up with his left. It was nice of him to take the time to visit the school loos, and to be honest I took his praise as a compliment. Nobody in the school could write poetry quite like me. Oh no, if this note didn't work, I'd hang up my Big Boy briefs and go and live in a monastery!

I slipped into the corridor and joined the rest of the school as they filed into assembly.

At the entrance to the hall, the queue hit a bottleneck and came to a shuddering halt. The weight of people pushing from behind squashed us together like figs in a fruit cake. As I was struggling to keep my hair above the shoulder of the boy in front, I felt a hand tug my elbow. I twisted round to see who it was and discovered that although my back had just enough space to turn, my legs were stuck fast pointing forwards. I heard several vertebrae click and realized I was temporarily stuck facing both ways at the same time, looking like a refugee from *The Exorcist*. But the worst was yet to come, for when I saw who had tugged my elbow, I felt the urge to vomit green bile. It was yucky Deborah Smeeton – Cyborg Girl. Half flesh, half metal and she was fluttering her eyes at me like a walrus with conjunctivitis.

"Hello, Johnny," she simpered, running her tongue over her thickly-moustachioed top lip.

"Oh, Debra," I said.

"De-BORE-ah, actually," replied my bespectacled reflection. We were standing nose to nose, chin to chin, lip to lip, and there was nothing I could do about it. She flicked her greasy pigtails out of my eyes and grinned at me, displaying the half-ton of metalwork which had recently been welded onto her teeth and made her look like she had a car crash in her mouth. "I don't know why people can't say my name right. Is that for me?" She was pointing at Alison's postcard which I was holding in my right hand.

"Er … no," I stammered, trying to push her away so I could breathe.

"Don't go," she insisted, pulling me back towards her. "I like it here."

"No really, I must!" I shouted, feeling a space open up in front of me. My back unwound like an elastic band and I span round in line with my legs.

"We must do that again sometime," giggled little Miss Metalmouth, running her finger up my back and trying for a tickling position under my arm. But I was too quick. I jerked away, sweating and lying in equal measures.

"Oh absolutely," I replied, darting through the gap in front of me. "Well, I'll be seeing you Debra."

"De-BORE-ah actually!" she called. But I'd already gone.

ON DEBORAH'S MOUTH

I don't want, I don't want, I don't want
To kiss her.
I do want, I do want, I do want
To miss her.
To start with, to start with

24

I can't kiss that face
'cause
I'd end up, I'd end up,
Stuck to her brace.

(Johnny Worms — for The News at
Ten in Nightmare City)

It was important to find a seat close to Alison, so that I could pass her my postcard. As I entered the hall, her hair band stood out like a jewelled crown, casting a golden aura round the third seat in on the seventh row. Cupid set his arrow and I flew across the hall towards my target, nudging my way into the row behind her by making all the younger kids shove up and share seats. At that moment the headmistress, Miss Bulstrode, appeared on stage and we all had to stand. Alison's hair rippled down her back as she rose, spreading such sweet perfume in my direction that I nearly fainted.

I caught a glimpse of Ginger on the other side of the hall, pretending to be sick at the sight of me mooning over Alison. I mouthed the word "baby!" at him, and attempted to illustrate my insult with an elaborate mime involving a sucking dummy and a disposable nappy. Unfortunately, that was the moment that the headmistress chose to tell the assembly to sit down, and while everyone else in the room did so, I was left standing on my own, giving Ginger's baby the full works; eyes closed, face puce, straining with every muscle in my body to fill the imaginary nappy around my waist.

"JOHNNY WORMS!" That was the headmistress' voice. I opened my eyes to find the whole school staring at me, including the teachers. My face burned up. I was squatting over my chair like a sumo wrestler and had to think fast. I smiled, then turned the strain into a cough, the squat into a sit, and pretended that the whole embarrassing incident had never happened, by whistling silently and studying the neon lights in the ceiling. The headmistress (God bless her!) resumed her address to the school on the current epidemic of nits.

After a decent pause, I leant forward and whispered "Alison," in Alison's ear, but Alison didn't respond, so I tried a little louder. "Alison!" She still didn't turn round, presumably because she hadn't heard me, but Timothy Winchester did. Funny how I hadn't noticed him there before, because Timothy Winchester was one of the largest boys in the school. He was as tall as he was wide, and as wide as he was thick. He was a human brick wall and he sat next to Alison in assembly to shield his beloved from the prying eyes of other boys. He thought she was his property, and he made this entirely clear by curling up

26

his bottom lip and growling at me. But the unstoppable sex machine was not to be deterred. I shunted the remedials up a couple more seats so I could touch Alison's shoulder. Then I leant over the back of her chair and dropped the postcard into her lap.

"If you don't cease these childish antics, Worms," said Timothy suddenly, keeping his eyes front, "I'll bloody your nose. Now jolly well push off." Timothy had a voice like a BBC newsreader and a knack for using the silliest words at the most inappropriate moments. I started to snigger.

"No, you jolly well push off," I mimicked, struggling to hold back my snorts of laughter. "I want to speak to Alison."

"JOHNNY WORMS" boomed the voice of the headmistress from the stage. "WHAT IS IT THAT YOU'VE GOT TO SAY THAT IS SO MUCH MORE FASCINATING THAN WHAT I'VE GOT TO SAY?" I looked innocently behind me, like she was talking to someone else. But there was only one Johnny Worms. "STAND UP AND TELL US ALL WHAT IT WAS YOU WERE SAYING." I stood up slowly. "WHAT WERE YOU TALKING ABOUT?" Now this was tricky. The absolutely last thing I wanted to do was to read my love postcard out loud in front of the entire school.

"Erm..." I wracked my brains for inspiration, but there was nothing there. "I was talking about…" I swallowed loudly. "Erm … Fish," I said.

"FISH!" came the retort. Why on earth had I said fish? I didn't know anything about fish, except that some of them had fingers, and now I'd got the whole school on tenterhooks, desperate to hear more.

"Yes, little fishy fish," I continued, pathetically, "with spots on." I was floundering. "And apparently they don't get nits, because they don't have any hair. Which is lucky for them, I'd say… So, erm … I was just saying… Excuse me, it's awfully hot in here. Would you mind if we opened a window?" The headmistress glowered her refusal. "Erm … I was just saying, what a pity it is that we aren't all fish … sort of thing." Now I might just have got away with this blarney had Timothy Winchester not stood up at that precise moment and waved my postcard in the air.

"Please, Miss Bulstrode," he announced in his beefy tones, "but I fear that Worms is not being entirely honest. I think this note which he just passed to the lovely Alison Mallinson…" (they exchanged tender glances) "might help you to discover his purpose in interrupting your most interesting and enlightening appraisal of the current nit epidemic."

"THANK YOU, TIMOTHY," said the headmistress. "JOHNNY WORMS WILL

NOW COME UP HERE AND READ US ALL HIS LETTER." Given the choice I would have preferred to eat my way through a boxful of live tarantulas, or even spend an afternoon kissing Deborah Smeeton, but the choice was not on offer. Public humiliation, however, was.

As I surveyed the sea of faces in front of me, from my elevated position on the teachers' platform, I was glad that I'd started Alison's note with a joke. At least a laugh would lighten my torture.

"You is the apple of my eye," I began. "Cor! I bet you taste good with custard!" There was nothing. Not a titter, not a cough, not a smile. "It was a joke," I explained, holding up my picture of the rotten apple. "Cor! ... Apple core?" One lone voice roared her approval and applauded my wit with gusto. But it wasn't Alison.

"THANK YOU, DEBRA," boomed the headmistress.

"De-BORE-ah actually," came the injured response, as she sat back down in her seat.

"DO CARRY ON, JOHNNY." I took a deep breath before entering the white water rapids of personal ignominy.

"Alison, Alison,
When can I see you some?
My heart is all cooked and done,
For a blinder called Alison (Mallinson)."

This time the school did laugh. It was a huge communal guffaw that spread out from Timothy Winchester at its centre, like a Mexican Wave. I blushed scarlet from head to toe and pretended that I had meant my card to be funny, but inside I was dying a thousand deaths. When at last the final wheeze had faded away and I considered my punishment over, the headmistress stood up and hammered the final nail into my coffin.

"BEFORE YOU GO!" she boomed. I stopped creeping off the stage and turned to face my tweed-suited tormentor.

"Yes?" I quaked.

"PERHAPS YOU'D LIKE TO TELL THE SCHOOL WHAT THE LETTERS S.W.A.L.K. STAND FOR." No, actually, no! I did not want to tell the school what the letters S.W.A.L.K. stood for, but the school it seemed was keen to know.

"Er... It's short for..." I giggled, nervously, "for ... er ... Sssssssss..." I couldn't bring myself to say the words. "Sssssssssss..." The school had all day. "Erm..." I took a run at it. "Sealed With A Loving Kiss!" There was uproar. The children threw themselves on the floor, banged their seats with their hands, and hooted like a poolful of sea lions. Timothy Winchester held Alison's hand as she bore the indignity with stoicism. Only her ears let her down, blushing a deep shade of pink around

their tips. Then, the headmistress thanked me
for being so entertaining and ordered me back
to my seat with the word "SEX-PEST" ringing
in my ears. I dragged my leaden feet back into
the well of the hall, through a barrage of cat-
calls, and imagined that I was taking my last,
long, lonely walk to the gallows.

At break, Alison sat apart from the other children on a shady bench at the far end of the
playground. She was icy cool, like a queen
amongst her courtiers, allowing only Timothy
to approach, to fawn upon her every whim
and soothe her troubled brow, while I was
trapped at the other end of the playground by
Deborah Smeeton.
  "I'll go out with you!" she panted, flashing
her broadest smile at me. The sun glinted off
her brace and dazzled me.
  "Sorry," I said. "That's out of the question."
  "Oh, go on!" she exhorted. "I love you!" I
had to nip her crush in the bud. I removed her
arms from around my neck.
  "Look, Debra…"
  "De-BORE-ah actually," came the prickly
reply.
  "Yes, look, if you and I went out with each
other it wouldn't be fair on Cecil."
  "Oh, please!" she exploded, scrunching her
face in disgust. "I don't love Cecil!"

"Oh!" said a tiny, shocked voice. Cecil had been standing behind her all the time.

"Go away!" admonished Deborah.

"No, don't!" I shouted, grabbing my spotty saviour before he could turn away. "She didn't mean it."

"Yes, I did," she replied, giving Cecil a sharp shove in the ribs to send him packing. "He does nothing but follow me round all day."

"That's because I like you," whispered the boy in the large yellow pompom hat, which his mother had knitted to ward off nits. "Do you like me?"

"No," said Deborah cruelly. "I like Johnny Worms. He's handsome." Cecil turned to me for support.

"Do you like me?" he asked. His huge eyelashes blinked like a moth's wings behind his thick-lensed spectacles.

"Very much, Cecil," I lied. I liked him about as much as I like those crusty lumps of ketchup that gather round the bottom of the lid.

"Do you want to come to my house for Christmas, then?" he said. I hesitated. "Or my birthday. It doesn't matter which. Mummy tookened me to see The *Three Bears on Ice* last year."

"And so does Debra," I jumped in. "Debra likes you too."

"De-BORE-ah!" screamed the little girl with pigtails. "It's De-BORE-ah for goodness'

32

sake. There's an O in the middle. Why won't people pronounce it?!" This kitten was starting to rattle my cage. It was time for some straight talking. I took my comb from my blazer pocket, ran it through my hair and squared off my shoulders.

"De-bore-ah," I snapped coldly, fixing her with my most steely stare. "You and I are finished." Deborah was stunned. She wasn't aware that we'd ever started. "Believe me, I know what's best for the both of us. Look after Cecil. He's a good man. You'll be happy together. But I'm not worth the pain. I'm a loner, always was, always will be." I chucked her under the chin. "Hey! No tears!" And I walked away. That was the way to do it. Cruel to be kind. They respected you for it in the end. But just as I thought I'd got away from her, I heard her scream, and when I looked round, Deborah Smeeton was swooning.

"He called me De-BORE-ah!" she dribbled, ecstatically. Then she collapsed to the ground and was given a rather wet kiss of life by Cecil Simpson.

"Something tells me," I muttered grimly, "that I haven't seen the last of Miss Tin-lips."

I hadn't seen the last of Timothy Winchester either. As I walked across the playground to join my class at "in-time", a large boot whoomfed me up the backside. Timothy's shadow loomed over me as I lay on the concrete. The loud lout brayed and recited a little poem of his own twittish making.

"Alison Mallinson
DON'T want to see you some.
Her heart's all cooked and done,
For a blinder called Timothy
Winchester.
Get it?"

"Thank you," I gasped. "That's very good. Only Winchester doesn't rhyme." And I braced myself for the second whoomf, which Timothy duly delivered, with all the upper-class subtlety of a steel-capped polo mallet.

ON TIMOTHY WINCHESTER

Huge and hairy,
Loud and scarey,
Bet his middle name's Mary,
The great big fairy!

(Johnny Worms — The pen is mightier than the boot)

While everyone else filed into class, Ginger stayed behind to help me up. I felt like a Canadian lumberjack had split me up the middle with a buzz saw.

"What is wrong with you?" chided Ginger. "I told you not to go near her."

34

"I'm not so sure I love her anymore," I winced, as I gently straightened my legs.

"I told you Winchester would have your guts for garters."

"He's had my nadgers for knickers, 'n' all," I moaned, throwing my right arm round Ginger's neck and tiptoeing, tentatively, towards the school entrance.

"Listen," he said, "I want you to hear what I'm saying now, OK?" He was speaking very slowly to make sure I got the point. "Football is good. Girls is bad. Trouble. Got it?"

"Got it," I said.

"So no more chasing girls."

"Sure," I said, gasping from the pain in my pelvis.

"And you'll give me a game of football after school?" I walked straight into that one. Ginger was always trying to get me to play when I didn't want to. I mean, heading the ball wreaks havoc with a cool hairdo and he won't let me play in a shower cap. I know, because I've asked him. Anyway, I said I'd play.

"Promise?" he said.

"Promise," I sighed. Just then someone lifted up my left arm and sneaked their head underneath.

"I'm not trouble, Johnny," slurped an all-too-familiar voice. "I love you!" That was the final straw. Deborah sent me hobbling into school screaming "Help!" at the top of my

voice, where I ran slap bang into the headmistress, who gave me a detention for being a
nuisance. Ginger wasn't so daft after all. Girls
IS trouble, even when they're women.

IN PRAISE OF FOOTBALL

Suddenly, it's all come clear,
It's girls who fill me full of fear.
It's football that I really likes
And Mates and Blokes and Motorbikes.
I'm starting from a new perspective,
Men First is my new directive.
No more chicks,
No more women,
No more chats 'bout thighs and slimmin'.
Just lots of great fun macho squabbles
'bout pubs and beards and manly
trubbles.
Oh yes, this really is the life
Thirteen years and still no wife!

(Johnny Worms — Now a confirmed
bachelor)

3
HOW SEXY ARE YOU?

After school, I had to wheel my bike home, because my sitting bits were too sore to sit on. Despite the crippling crutch cramps, I was quite enjoying the walk. Something fundamental had flipped over in my head. Life was much less confusing now I didn't have to worry about women anymore.

I turned into my road and teetered past Mr Patel's glittering corner shop. I had always admired Mr Patel and thought him to be a shopkeeper of exceptional brain. He had very cleverly, in my opinion, called his shop "The Shop Here Please Shop", so that all you could see as you came up the street were the three words SHOP HERE PLEASE emblazoned in ten-foot letters across the shiny red awning. Today there was an additional banner strung across the front of the shop which proudly

37

announced that digestive biscuits were "Down!
Down! Down! to only 37p."

"Good afternoon," I called, as I minced
past. Mr Patel was standing outside his empo-
rium flicking a pink feather duster over three
buckets of cut flowers.

"Tell me about it," he grumbled. "What is
so very good about it, please? I have just been
making a lot of thoroughly wise investments
and nobody wants to be knowing, thank you."
He indicated two brand new vending machines
that were standing outside the shop next to a
racked display of freezer clips for sealing
bags of frozen peas. I'd seen similar-looking
machines in pictures of gambling casinoes in
Las Vegas.

"What do they do?" I asked. Mr Patel point-
ed to the glass-fronted one, which contained a
red plastic chicken brooding on a pile of blue
eggs.

"Prizes for all the family," he said, unen-
thusiastically. "Much fun to be had from the
clucking hen, but nobody want to have a
go. Only 20p to boot." To be honest, the
chicken looked a bit babyish, but the second
machine was right up my street. It was like
a "Speak Your Weight Machine" only it had
a fake fur trim and a picture of a cute, curvy
lady in a bikini sprayed across its neon-stud-
ded front. She was gorgeous, even if she was
just a painting.

"How Sexy Are You?" said Mr Patel.

"Well, I've never had any complaints," I replied, thinking it a bit of a funny question for him to ask. Mr Patel corrected my misunderstanding.

"No. "How Sexy Are You?" machine. Hours of fun for forty pence. You want a try, please?" I was intrigued, of course (not that I needed a machine to tell me how sexy I was, not when I had a bathroom mirror at home), and I was all for saying yes, when suddenly I remembered that I'd just made a vow to give up women for good.

"Sorry," I said. "I can't." But Mr Patel was not Local Businessman of the Year for nothing. He had sold rubbish bags to the dustbinmen and he could see that I was interested enough to be a potential sale.

"No, please. Just one try, Johnny. Without it you will never be knowing just how sexy you really are, and believe me the ladies will be wanting to have that information."

"Not any more," I said, piously. "I'm a bachelor."

"No, no, listen... If you aren't finding out today, you will be sitting all alone when you are a very crusty old man with no one to care for you. You will be cold and poor, and you will be looking back and thinking, why was I not listening to my most wise chum, Mr Patel? If I had known that I was so sexy, I could have married and been blessed with very many lots of children who would be looking after me now in my old age."

"Yeah, but women is trouble, Mr Patel," I said, revelling in the fact that this was the first proper man's talk I'd ever had. "I mean, do I really want to get back in the ring with them? I don't think so."

"Loving is not a boxing match," Mr Patel said, slightly confused.

"It is when you cross Timothy Winchester." I winced and I went on to explain my dilemma with Alison. He was very sympathetic and shook his head sorrowfully as I told him how I had tried in vain to touch her soul. When I'd finished, he put his hand on my shoulder.

"Johnny, sir, you are having a very nasty dose of the Lady Blues. Only one known cure in the whole wide world that I know of." He paused to bring my attention to a peak. "One go on the "How Sexy Are You?" machine, to be putting back all the confidence in yourself."

"But I've only got sixty-seven pence."

"Only sixty-seven pence? The gods are smiling on you! You can be having not only one go on the "How Sexy Are You?" machine, but also one gift from the clucking hen. It's a miracle, and you will still be having a Princely seven pence change!"

"Forget the hen," I said, "and you've got a deal." You know how it is when you make a resolution, but secretly you know you're not going to stick to it. I'd never tell Ginger, but that's how I felt when I promised him I'd given up girls. It's like peanut butter, I couldn't give that up either. So I caved in, said yes, felt a hundred times better and shoved the index finger of my right hand into the small metal collar on top of the "How Sexy Are You?" machine. I inserted my forty pence and the machine burst into life. A rubber pad vibrated under my finger as it played a tinny version of "I'm too sexy for my car". Then a yellow sign lit up on the neon panel in front of me, indicating that I was so unsexy I ought to TRY PUTTING A PAPER BAG OVER YOUR HEAD. "Very good machine," chortled Mr Patel. "This is most exciting!" Actually, it was more terrifying than exciting, because the vibrations from the pad had started to spread outwards and the machine was rocking backwards and forwards on its base. The yellow sign had turned orange and now said SEXYISH.

"Is this meant to happen?" I asked, nervously.

"You must be very sexy boy," replied Mr Patel, as the sign turned deep orange and informed me that I was a LATIN LOVER. "I am thinking that the machine is liking you." The machine was now shaking me so hard that I was jiggling from head to toe like an electric eel in a toaster.

41

"There's s...s...smoke c...c...coming out the b...b...back!" I screamed as the machine left the ground and danced across the pavement. A bell rang somewhere inside the lady's bikini as the sign turned crimson and flashed RED HOT SEX POT.

"Oh dear! Take your finger out and be quick!" shouted Mr Patel. But it was a bit late for that. With a bang and a whizz and an electronic crunch, the back of the machine exploded and sent a shower of sparks all over Mr Patel's freezer clips, which melted instantly. My hair was sticking up like a fir cone and my finger was smoking like a Colt 45. I felt all warm and woosey and my face kept cracking into an inane grin.

"Wow!" I gasped. Mr Patel had buried himself behind the machine to check for damage, and was muttering loudly.

"If I had been knowing that I was asking Johnny bloody Casanova to stick his whotsit into my machine, I would not have been so damned encouraging."

"Who's this Casanova?" I asked.

"The man who made love to more women in one week than most men see in a lifetime. The sexiest man in the whole universe ever!" I was impressed.

"So you think I'm the sexiest boy in the whole universe ever?" Mr Patel was making a strange clicking noise in the back of his throat and staring sadly at the blackened plug in his hand.

"No. I am thinking that maybe I put the wires in back to front! Oh dear! Oh dear, oh dear!" And with that, he retreated into his shop to console himself with a bag of jelly babies. I, on the other hand, had just had three hundred volts shot through my nervous system and was pulsating with animal magnetism; hip-hopping with hairy-arsed hormones. My libido rose from the dead – like Frankenstein's monster – and once again I became the unstoppable sex machine!

ON THE IMPORTANCE OF NAMES

The name what bowls the ladies over
Is the one of Casanova.
I wonder if the name of Worms
Makes the ladies think of germs?

(Johnny Worms — in the middle of an identity crisis)

4
PURPLE PASSION

I was standing on the pavement buzzing like a faulty street lamp and grinning like a monkey in a bowl of nuts when Ginger rode up on his bike. He'd been home, changed and pumped up his football.

"There you are," he said. I went round your house, but you weren't there."

"I was here," I said.

"I can see that for myself," said Ginger. "You ready?"

"Sure," I lied. How was I going to tell him about the "How Sexy Are You?" machine and that I'd given up football and switched back to girls again? He'd think I was fickle. We cycled in silence for a minute or so before I took the plunge.

"Ginger," I started. "What would you think if I changed my name to Casanova?"

"Why?" he said.

"Oh, nothing," I replied and then added boldly, "it's a lover's name, that's all," hoping he'd catch my drift.

"It sounds like ice-cream with green bits in," he mocked, but I ignored his ignorance and took the bit between the teeth.

"I've got something to tell you, mate."

"I've got it sorted," he said. "You, me and Safraz, against Dean, Kieran and that fat bloke in Mr Whybrow's class. We'll wipe the floor with them."

"Yeah, about the football..." I persisted.

"What do you reckon, ten nil?" There was no easy way to say this.

"I'm still in love," I said.

"Fifteen?"

"I still love Alison Mallinson. It's like a mind drug. I want to marry her!" Ginger skidded his bike into the pavement.

"What? But you said..."

"I know what I said," I said, crashing into his back wheel, "but I've just bust the "How Sexy Are You?" machine and it's cleared my mind. You see, the way I reckon it is that some of us are born filthy, brutish footballers – that's you, Ginger – and others, like me, we're made of finer stuff; soft and gentle, loving and caring. Men who shave off their beards 'cause it gives their girlfriends a rash when they kiss them."

"You haven't got a beard," scoffed Ginger.

"I have! Look." I pulled down my top lip and thrust it into his face. "Feel that."

"That's skin," he said, prodding it with his finger.

"That's a five o'clock shadow," I retorted, angrily.

"One o'clock," he sneered.

"Yeah, all right, so it's a bit faint at the moment, but with a bit of shaving it'll flow like a billy goat's." I peered into the mirror on my handlebars just to check that I was right, but Ginger did seem to have a point. My top lip was definitely peachy. I turned my head to see if there was any other sign of growth and was preparing for the worst when the sun came out and lit up my right ear. "Look!" I shouted. "Look, I've got sideburns." In front of my ear was a tiny patch of soft, white down. "I've got proper sideburns and I'm not even fourteen yet!"

"Timothy Winchester's already shaving," Ginger mocked.

"I don't care," I said. "I'm not going to kiss ape-boy Winchester, am I?" Ginger shook his head.

"You'll never learn, will you? He'll kill you good and proper this time."

"Nothing can keep us apart, Ginger. Alison and I were made for each other. It's written in the stars." (I'd read that bit in one of Mum's magazines.) "Love conquers all, mate, even Timothy Winchester!"

Ginger crammed his fist down his throat and pretended to puke.

"You never listen to what I say," he sulked. "I'm off to kick a ball around." He pushed his bike away from the kerb and left me to follow.

"Ginger!" I shouted, struggling to catch up. "She's the girl of my dreams!" But Ginger had closed his ears. I'd betrayed my best mate and he was hurting.

We travelled in silence again. Up Shooter's Hill, right past the duck pond and left into Nelson's Way, a perfectly ordinary suburban street, filled with rows of perfectly ordinary mock Tudor houses, filled with rows of perfectly ordinary people, watering their stone windmills and polishing their front lawns. We were halfway down the street when it happened. It was 4.32 and it struck out of the blue like a thunderbolt, only it was a she.

It was Ginger who noticed her first, because he was two hundred yards ahead of me when she pulled out in front of him.

"Watch it!" he shouted, as his front wheel scraped against her rear mudguard and he bounced up the kerb. He hit a lamppost and flew forward out of his saddle, fetching himself a painful crack on the vertical strut of his handlebars. She didn't say sorry. She didn't say anything. She was a cool drool. She just pulled across the road and started cycling towards me.

My eyes were hurting on account of her beauty. She was a two-wheeled vision in purple. Long blonde hair, thick, wrinkled, black tights and a sultry look on her face that said "Don't Touch or I'll Whack You With My D-Lock". She was ravishing, sitting upright in her saddle, her school books buried in the basket in front of her like a litter of soft, brown puppies, the buttons on her purple uniform glinting in the sunshine. She was chewing a piece of bubblegum and blowing huge pink bubbles out the side of her mouth, which is a trick I really admire in a woman.

She wobbled slightly to avoid a pothole and I shot her a wry, let's-share-this-amusing-little-incident-together smile, pushing my head forward to give her the best possible view of my sideburns, but she must have been momentarily distracted, because she didn't notice me. What I wouldn't have given for the courage to raise my arm and call out to her, "Hi, doll, Johnny's the name, big loving's the game!" but my tongue wouldn't move and my lips were set fast in a gormless grin. And that was the sum total of our first meeting. Insignificant on the surface but devastating underneath. That she didn't look at me could only have meant one thing. She wanted me, sure, but she was too shy to ask. She had old-fashioned values, expected the man to make the first move. Only trouble was, I wasn't sure how to do it.

It was seeing Ginger hopping about on the pavement that gave me the idea. When I saw her again, I'd wait until she was alongside me before staging a tragic bike crash. I'd pretend to swerve to avoid a cat and throw myself off my bike into the gutter. She couldn't fail to notice that. Then, I'd just lie there groaning – manly groans, no soppy whimpering – and softly call out for help in a cracked voice that hinted at imminent death from internal bleeding. She'd leap from her bike, rush to my side and bend down to cradle my head in her arms. "Oh, Heavens above!" she'd say. "This is a tragedy! Don't die! Not now, when we've only just met." I'd look up at her through misty eyes and smile weakly. "Why did it have to take this to bring us together?" And she'd stroke my forehead tenderly and brush her hair across my cheek. "I know that I'm two years older than you and that your voice hasn't broken yet, but it doesn't matter. Let the world disapprove. What do we care when we have each other!" "And our love!" I'd add, smiling weakly again and pursing my lips together in readiness for the kiss which would surely follow! "And our love!" she'd reply, panting ever so slightly, as her budding breasts shuddered with budding emotion. And then we would kiss, and then I'd jump up, pretend that I was much better now, thanks to her nursing, exchange phone numbers and, bob's your uncle, we'd be stepping out!

But that was for next time. Right now, I'd missed her.

WHAT I WANT TO KNOW

How come girls have got those
hormones,
That turn boys into gibb'ring
morones?
What's it about
A woman's pout,
That turns a man who's capable
Into a mushy vegetable?

(Johnny Worms — head over-cooked in
love)

Ginger was gasping for breath and clutching his floppy bits when I pulled up next to him.

"Stupid girl," he squeaked, in a slightly higher voice than usual. "Damn near killed me. Why doesn't she look where she's going?"

"Yeah," I said, moonily. "Wasn't she beautiful?" Ginger stopped clutching himself and looked at me like I was some sort of Martian.

"Oh, no," he said. "You're not in love with her as well, are you?"

"I think I am, Ginger."

"Blimey, if you were a cat, I'd have you done at the vet's. I mean, what about Alison? Ten minutes ago, you two were getting married!"

"Well, I hadn't met my vision in purple then, had I? Alison's history, Ginge, just a faded phone number in my battered address book." Ginger blew a disapproving raspberry and picked his bike up off the pavement.

"You should wear a sign round your neck," he said, "with IN LOVE on one side and NOT IN LOVE on the other, then I'd know where I stood with you."

"What's the matter?" I protested. "I thought you'd be pleased. It was you who said I should dump Alison."

"Yeah, for football, not another bird!"

"I can't help falling in love," I said.

"That's the problem; you fall in love, but they don't seem to fall in love back, do they?"

"Give it time," I said. "I'm not called the unstoppable sex machine for nothing." That was when Ginger, being the sensitive soul that he is, showed me two fingers.

"You promised," he said bitterly. "You promised to play." He was standing astride his cross bar looking so utterly miserable that I couldn't let him down again.

"Of course I did," I said, "and I meant it. Come on! Let's go duff up Dean, Kieran and that fat bloke from Mr Whybrow's class!"

That was all he wanted to hear and he forgave me on the spot. We sped off down the road, chanting "Ten nil, ten nil, ten nil, ten nil," until we thought our lungs would burst.

A PASSIONATE POEM ABOUT PURPLE

Purple's the colour of violets,
The colour of rain and of plums.
It's also the colour of luv bites
which we'll both have to hide from our
mums.

(Johnny worms — for my very own
purple heart)

We lost the match 24 – 1. It turned out that the fat bloke from Mr Whybrow's class plays for the Crystal Palace Youth Team and is tipped to be an England striker one day.

"You were useless," sulked Ginger, who'd stopped the game early by taking his ball back.

"I scored a goal," I reminded him.

"At OUR end!" he shrieked. "Every time I put you in on their goal you missed, because you were gazing up at the sky."

"Sorry," I said. "The clouds reminded me of Purple's soft, white dimples."

"Soppy git," he said. "I'm not playing with you again."

"OK," I said casually. Ginger took off his shoe and threw it at me and I suddenly realized he was as close to crying as I'd ever seen him. He charged at me like a windmill uprooted by a hurricane, both fists flailing, striking me as often and as hard as he could about the head and shoulders.

"I really hate you sometimes!" he screamed.

"Ginger!" I didn't know what had got into him. I guess the match must have meant more to him than I'd realized.

"You and your bloody girls!" he shouted. "I wish you were all dead."

"What you on about? Stop it. Ginger, stop it!" I tried to catch his fists and pin his arms to his sides. "They're only girls! You're my mate!" But Ginger had broken away and was stomping back to his bike. And they *were* only girls, but I still quite liked them. "You've forgotten your shoe," I called out as he disappeared behind a tree.

I found him with his head in his hands. He didn't want me to see that he'd been crying. I sat down beside him on the damp grass and pushed his shoe into his lap.

"Sorry," I said. "I wasn't much cop out there, was I?" He turned his body away from me. His shoe tumbled to the floor. "It's all a bit muddled up in my head, you see, Ginger. I thought I loved Alison, but now I don't, because I've met another woman." He still wouldn't speak. "I like football, really I do."

"I hurt my foot," he muttered, wiping his nose on his sleeve. "Trod on something."

"Any blood?" I asked.

"Dunno," he said. "Haven't looked."

"Can't see any," I said. "Look, I want you to know that even though I am in love with that girl in the purple uniform, I'm still your mate first, OK?" He grunted something which sounded like OK and I picked up his shoe.

"Girls muck up football," mumbled Ginger. "If you go back to Alison, I won't be your best friend anymore." And that was about as clear as he could make it. "Come on," he said suddenly, standing up and stuffing his foot into his laced shoe. "I'm bored with this." So was I. So, we got on our bikes and went home. On the way I asked him if he thought Purple thought I was sexy, but he didn't answer, so I didn't ask again.

FAREWELL TO ALISON

Purple's
Immurtal
But
Alison's
Dead.

(Johnny Worms — telling it like it is)

5
THE WAR ZONE

I arrived home to find Mum and Uncle Stan searching for a button underneath the kitchen table. I knew that's what they were doing crawling around on the floor, because Mum told me.

"Hello, Johnny," she said. "We didn't expect you back so early. Me and Uncle Stan were just looking for a button under the table." Uncle Stan then repeated everything that Mum had just said, presumably to make sure I'd understood. I told him, of course I'd understood, but that seemed to make him even more agitated.

"Why? What did you think we were doing?" he challenged.

"Well, looking for a button," I said. "It must be a jolly precious one for all the fuss you're making!" Mum and Uncle Stan just grunted, as if losing the button in the first place

55

was all my fault. Then Stan got up and left. "Good day, pumpkin?" my mum enquired as she flattened her hair and rearranged her apron. "Pull up a seat and I'll cook you some smashing eggs."

Five minutes later, a pall of black smoke billowed from the frying pan and hung over our heads, like we were living in a war zone. Dad came in in a really bad mood and when Mum said, "Oh, look at Mr Sulky Pants. Left your smile in your briefcase, did you?" it just made matters worse. He muttered something about Uncle Stan the Do-It-All Man and slumped down on his chair at the far end of the table with his copy of *Gnome Monthly*. Mum lit a cigarette and blew the smoke into his face. Dad hated that and she knew it.

"I do wish you wouldn't smoke in front of the children," he coughed through clenched teeth.

"I do wish you wouldn't come in here and read your magazine instead of talking to me," replied Mum.

"Well, I wish you wouldn't keep telling me to stop coming in here and reading my magazine instead of talking to you."

"Well, I wish you wouldn't hold your little finger out when you sip your tea."

"And I hate your slippers," added Dad.

"And me, your jumper," said Mum.

"Bleurgh!"

"Bleurgh!"

They could go on like this for hours, but today it was Mum who got the last word in.

"And I loathe the way you tuck your napkin into your collar!" She took another drag on her fag and wiped the smudged eye make-up off her cheek. Dad tucked his napkin firmly into his collar, buried his head in his magazine, and mumbled, "Fine, I see," and created a huge silence, which was only broken by a squeal from Mum.

"Ooh heck, me eggs!" The frying pan was on fire, spitting red flames up the cherry-patterned wall tiles. Dad had had enough. His head disappeared inside the low-lying cloud of burnt sunflower oil as he stood up and polished his glasses.

"No tea today," he said. "I'm off. Got to check my gnomes before it gets dark."

Dad's collection of gnomes lived in the garden shed, next to his model railway set. Short ones, fat ones, red ones, green ones. Some with little fishing rods, some with wooden wheelbarrows and one with a pair of football boots around his neck. This was Norman (named after Norman Hunter), Dad's pride and joy. "Mind you keep that dog off Norman," he always said as he left of a morning. "If I come home to find he's buried him in the compost heap, there'll be hell to pay!" Dad was Norman-mad and today was

Norman's twenty-first birthday. He stopped at the door and came back to the table, holding a tiny black and white stone football in his hand. "I meant to show you this, kids," he said. "Norman's birthday present. Do you think he'll like it?"

"Yeth," said Sherene, "'cauthe I love football too, 'cauthe it'th not a thilly girly game where they make you wear big, baggy, brown knickerth!" I thought the stone ball was daft, but I didn't dare say it, because Dad had mellowed at the mention of Norman, and I didn't want to put him back in a bad mood.

"By the way, that reminds me," he said, "you haven't forgotten what tomorrow is, have you?" I stared at Sherene and she stared at me. "You have, haven't you?" said my dad. It certainly looked that way, but if we said nothing Dad would never know.

"Ith it pocket money day?" asked Sherene, proving just how thick little sisters are. Dad's lips tightened like a woodlouse curling up into a ball. There was trouble brewing.

"Oh, tomorrow," I stalled, taking evasive action. "Yeah, don't you worry Dad, we'll be there."

"Where?" he said. Now he was testing me.

"At the ... er ... important event." I winked. I didn't know what I was winking about. I was just hoping that if I could blather on for long enough, Dad might give up and go to his shed.

"You don't know, do you?"

"'Course I do," I lied. "I mean, it's just, like, you know, we want to keep it a secret, don't we? Eh? Tomorrow. The big day. Secret. Just between ourselves... Tomorrow." The suspense was too much for Mum.

"What secret's this?" she squeaked. "What you planning for my birthday, then?" Dad groaned.

"IT'S MUM'S BIRTHDAY!" I shouted, over-enthusiastically. "I hadn't forgotten that." But Dad knew that I had and left the kitchen with a face as black as a sour plum.

"Ignore him," said Mum. "He's just an old grouch, pumpkins. Grub's up!" And she scraped four charcoaled eggs out of the pan, clattering them onto our plates like oil-sluiced hubcaps. Fortunately, Pongo chose that moment to parp throatily, which meant that we had to evacuate and didn't have to eat them.

Sherene followed me into the lean-to and hovered like she had something important to tell me.

"What are you doing here?" I asked. "You should be upstairs having a bath."

"If you had to thave the world," she started.

"Oh, not this again."

"No, if you had to thave the world, would you put your nothe next to Pongo'th bottom?"

"But I don't have to save the world, do I?"

"No, but if you HAD to!" screamed my little sister, whose very life depended on knowing my answer.

"If I HAD to," I mimicked, "then, yes, I would put my nose next to Pongo's bottom." Sherene scrunched up her lips till they looked like a prune.

"Ugh! Ugh! Ugh!" she grimaced. "You are dithGUTHTING!" Then she raced indoors, shaking her head and spitting out some imagined foulness. "Mummy! Do you know what Johnny wantth to do to Pongo?" It was nothing to what I wanted to do to her! I jumped on my bike and shot off to Mr Patel's to get Mum a birthday present. Suddenly his clucking hen machine didn't seem so daft after all. "Prizes for all the family... Only 20p!" Well, Mum was family, so a cheap blue plastic egg would do her nicely.

As my back wheel skidded off the pavement, a curtain twitched in our attic window. It was our Nan, waving goodbye from her rooftop prison. In her hands she was holding a faded velveteen birthday card that she'd stolen from WH Smith on November 15th 1973. Ever since that day, she'd been convinced that the police were coming to get her. That was why she stayed locked in the attic. My dad occasionally lured her out by laying a trail of chocolate raisins down the stairs, but she was happier when hiding. I could see her lips moving now, slowly, like she was talking underwater, and even though I couldn't hear what she was saying, I knew exactly what it was, because I'd heard it a million times before.

"That's all right, officer, it's a fair cop. I'll come quietly!" She put her wrists together and held them out towards me. Then she smiled, showing the gaps in her teeth. "You couldn't give us a kiss first, though, could you?"

Barking mad my family, the lot of them!

ON FAMILIES AND GROWING UP

There's nothing more embarrassing,
When into school you's forced to bring
Your next of kin to see your work.
They make you feel an utter berk!
Kissing you in front of chums,
Singing over other mums,
Or cheering when you miss a kick,
And telling teachers why you're sick.
"He's got a boil upon his arse
The size of that Mount Everast!"
I think if I could change my lot,
I'd change the family what I've got.

(Johnny Worms — wishing he was older
and could leave home)

6

THE LANGUAGE OF LOVE

"Oh, Master Johnny Casanova, it is a perfectly lovely gift and will truly be making her weep buckets," said Mr Patel, when I unscrewed the freshly laid, blue egg and discovered a cheap brooch inside. "If you close your eyes you could believe those stones were diamonds!" he added, excitedly. I closed my eyes, but still believed the stones were plastic. I didn't tell Mr Patel though. I didn't want to upset him.

Mum was standing at the sink, chipping black bits off the saucepan with a chisel, when I re-entered the kitchen.

"Where've you been?" she said.

"It's a secret!" I grinned, patting the brooch in my pocket. "By the way," I added casually, "Mr Patel thinks I'm like Casanova." I wanted to see if a woman's reaction to the name would be different to Ginger's.

"Now, he's a nice man," she drooled all suggestively.

"I think so," I replied. "His biscuits are cheap at the moment."

"Not Mr Patel," she said, "Giovanni Casanova. I wouldn't mind him for a birthday present."

"Why?" I asked, but for some reason this seemed to embarrass her and she changed the subject.

"Remind me to do your hair with this nit lotion before bed," she said, brandishing a bottle of thick, yellow liquid with a skull and crossbones on the label. I wasn't having that lotion within seven million miles of my sacred hair. It probably contained acid or something to dissolve the nits' body armour. So I said,

"It's all right. I haven't got nits. Don't need it," and left the kitchen double quick, before she could get her hands out of the sink and delouse me on the spot.

On the way home from Mr Patel's, I'd decided that what I really needed to break the ice with Purple was a love poem, something that I could chuck at her as our bikes crossed paths. I was heading for my bedroom to wrestle with the muse, when I tripped over a long-faced Sherene, lying flat out on the landing and stubbing her toes into the carpet.

"Go away!" she said, grumpily. "I'm thulking."

"I'm allowed to walk across the landing, aren't I?" I snapped back. "This is my home too, you know!" She humphed and squeaked as if the whole world was set against her.

"Daddy thayth I've got to do a card for Mummy'th birthday, and I don't know what to dwaw." I suggested a house. "Oh yeth, that would be exciting, wouldn't it! Hip hip hooray, Shewene'th dwawn a pwetty little houthe. Let'th pat her on the head and give her a pink wibbon! I want to dwaw a shark or thomething. Or a twactor with lionth on the back, or a naeroplane with itth engine on fire, but I can't."

"Why not?" I asked.

"Lithen here," hissed my baby sister. "If you were going to die ... a weally howwible death, I mean..."

"Oh, not again," I groaned.

"No lithen. IF you were going to die weally howwibly, and thomebody thaid, 'Hello, little boy, I can thave you, but you have to be a girl, firtht.' What would you do?"

"I'd be a girl," I said without hesitation. "What a daft question."

"I knew you'd thay that, 'cauthe you're a pig. I wouldn't. I wouldn't be a girl if they thmacked me, or thwew eggth at me, or anything. I hate being a girl, 'cauthe girlth have to

64

dwaw thmelly houtheth for their Mummy'th birthdayth and I WANT TO DWAW A SHARK, WITH BLOOD!"

"So dwaw one!" I said. "Draw one, I mean." I couldn't understand why she was getting so upset.

"But I can't," she bawled, thumping the carpet with her fists. "I can only dwaw houtheth!" Sherene was unfathomable. I couldn't understand her from one mood swing to the next. I could only hope that my Purple Goddess was made of simpler stuff, otherwise I'd never find the key to unlock the secrets of her heart.

A snorting and a snuffling outside my door told me that Pongo wanted to come in. I had made it clear to him that he was not welcome in my bedroom unless he maintained a stricter control of his slurry-filled sphincter, but Pongo was a dog and didn't understand long words. So while I lay on my bed, jotting down the odd rhyming couplet for Purple, lost in tender thoughts of wild red roses, peach-coloured sunsets and creamy white chocolates, I heard the old bloodhound nudge open the door and sneak into my bedroom. Luckily for the wizened, woofing windbag, love was my overriding emotion at that precise moment and I couldn't bring myself to chuck him out. He dropped down on to his stomach and

65

crawled along the floor until he was underneath my bed, whereupon he collapsed with exhaustion, compressed his bowel by mistake and phooted like a rhinoceros. Fortunately, my poetic inspiration was unaffected by Pongo's critical flatulence.

> You should know, dear,
> That when you're near, dear,
> I'm a thousand miles from Hell!
> Yes, it's true, luv,
> It's you that I luv,
> Cor blimey, what's that smell?

Well maybe Pongo's gassy gutful did intrude on my thoughts after all, but not for long. By the time the canine fug had lifted, I had penned another lyrical masterpiece.

> Fertle Purple
> You make my heart sing.
> Fertle Purple
> You make my bell ring.
> Fertle Purple
> You's the one I adore,
> So Fertle Purple
> Let's snog on the floor.

On reflection, it was still not quite there. And then suddenly I had it. Like a cloud of white doves bursting over a hilltop, like a tidal wave smashing through serried rows of cobwebbed beach huts, like a lightbulb being switched on, it came to me. Something straight out of Lord Byron's top drawer.

True luv does never end sometimes.

It was perfect.

I wrote the sentence out neatly on a piece of card and drew an arrow and a heart next to it. At the top of the arrow I printed "To My Purple Goddess", and at the bottom I wrote the name "J. Casanova". Mum's sparkly eyed reaction had been the clincher. I'd grown sick of the name Worms. It was a slimy turn-off and the reason why I'd never had any luck with girls. But Casanova would change all that. There'd be cheerleaders beating a path to my door, whole hockey teams lining up to see me in the bath, even Princess Diana would find me hopelessly irresistible, probably. For the moment, though, Johnny Casanova only had to attract Purple and attract her he would, when she received the card tomorrow. I sealed my purple prose in a pink envelope, hurriedly wrapped Mum's birthday brooch in an old torn comic and retired early to bed, to wallow in purple-tinted daydreams about my beloved. As my head hit the pillow, however, I fell straight to sleep without even recalling what she looked like.

ON THE EFFECT OF POEMS ON
GIRLS

If a girl don't like your poem
It's confirmed, she's not worth
knowin'

(Johnny Casanova — Poet Lorry Hat
to the Queen)

7
YOUNG LOVE'S DREAM

I am sitting in the barber's chair, blue bib tucked into my collar, hands on knees, waiting for the lock-chopping to begin. My mum is sitting on a red metal foldaway chair by the window, pretending to read last week's Daily Star. *The barber is standing between us awaiting instructions, his bushy Greek moustache twitching with undisguised irritation.*

"Well?" he says.

"I want it cut long," I say loudly and first, to take the wind out of Mum's sails.

"Short," she snaps. "Short back and sides!" Her puffy, green eyes stare daggers at me over the top of the newspaper headline: MUM ABANDONS SON IN CROCODILE PARK. It's giving her ideas.

"But it's my hair," I protest. "It's sacred."

"Don't be silly, Johnny. Tombs are sacred, not those lanky rats' tails that you call hair."

69

This is one of those turning points in a young man's life and the barber knows it. Will I do what Mum wants or please myself? It's like a David Attenborough film. The moment when the fledgling teeters on the edge of the nest before making its first flight, or the joey leaves the warmth of its pouch, or the baby whale bonds with a submarine and heads off into the deep blue waters of the Persian Gulf with its newfound love. That moment of indecision before the plunge. It's history in the making. Long or short? Which way will the scissors fall?

"Long," I say. "Inch off, max!" There is steel in my eyes. The barber gulps. His Adam's apple runs up and down his hairy throat like a ferret in a pair of woollen trousers, and my mum gets up and leaves.

Now there's just me, the Greek and Pongo left. Pongo flops on to his back and rips off a snorter that scatters tiny droplets of muttish moisture into the four corners of the shop, and suddenly there's no need to damp down my hair. The barber takes his hands out of his pockets while I show him how much I want off and I get the shock of my life. He's got the shakes. Fingers that dance about on the end of his arms like a fistful of bop-crazy bananas. Trembling hands into which I am entrusting my sacred locks! Not such a good idea. No, I think I'll just get up and follow my mum out,

*but Sweeney Todd is twisting my head
towards his quivering scissors.*

*"Oh, yes," I shout jovially, trying to get up
out of the chair. "That looks great. You've
done a really good job. Well, I'll be off then."
He pushes me back into the seat with his
shaking hand.*

*"I no done nothing yet. Don't move!" he
orders. I don't dare. With both of us moving,
casualties would be unavoidable. He clenches
his fingers around my neck and straightens his
arm, using it like a laser beam to guide the
scissors on to my hair.*

*"Actually..." I start to say, but I'm too late.
I can feel the cold steel on the fleshiness of my
ear-lobes. It's about as safe as a hip-high
scythe in a men-only sauna.*

*After a while I get used to it. I close my eyes
and pretend I'm not there and after a count of
ten I'm not. I'm running down a corridor into
a black hole where the barber's voice becomes
sort of woolly round the edges, like one of
those old Movietone newsreaders, who didn't
have microphones and recorded their words
on thick, white candles by speaking into tin
cans. The vibrating barber is shouting,*

*"Don't move your head. I said, don't... on't
... on't ... on't moo ... moo ... moo ... moo ...
move your head ... head ... head ... head ...
head ... head." He sounds like he's standing in
a huge cave and I can't resist having a go*

myself, to see if I'm in there with him.

"Mary had a little lamb,
Its fleece was old and smelly,
And when the barber cut it off
He slipped and nicked its belly ... belly ...
belly ... belly."

I am. And then I'm not. I'm back in the shop
and the barber's showing me the back of my
head in a mirror, and my mum and dad are
both there, dressed up to the nines in dinner
jackets and pearls and shaking the barber's
hand for a job well done. They would think
that. I'm bald. He's shaved me down to the last
follicle. Not a sprout of sacred hair for miles!
But when I turn around to scream blue
murder, the whole shop disappears, along
with the street and my mum and dad, and I'm
standing on the step outside "Miss Ballan-
tyne's Ballet School for Nice Young Girls"
with my finger on the doorbell and a draught
round my ears that wasn't there half an hour
before.

I'm thirteen years old, I'm a serious slap-
head and I'm about to pas de deux *with a*
bunch of six-year-old girls. This could spell the
end of my reputation. And I'm thinking; what
happens if someone sees me? Or worse, what
happens if that someone is Alison Mallinson?
Or just any girl, come to that, but mainly
Alison, because I love her brains as well as her
looks (but mainly her looks).

"Johnny?" I recognize the voice immediately and my stomach turns to spinach soup. *"Johnny Casanova, is that you?"* And there she is, Alison Mallinson, with her come-hither eyes, soft pouting lips and a thick, black mane of hair tumbling down to her waist like a shimmering oil slick. And here's me with a bald head. No chance! *"What are you doing, Johnny?"* she whispers. Her voice drips chocolate ice cream down the back of my neck. *"I thought we had a date."* I have to sit down. A date with Alison! My head is swimming while my body drowns. And I forgot it?! A date with Alison is not the sort of thing you forget. The whole male population of Crawley wants to go out with Alison Mallinson and I forget!

"I forgot," I say, regretting the words instantly, as her luscious mouth quivers. *"I mean, I'm waiting for my sister to come out from ballet class. I forgot that I had to pick her up."*

"That's sweet," she says.

"Not half as sweet as you, baby," says a voice inside my head.

"We'll wait together then," she continues. So, I'm standing next to her with my mouth open, trying to look all sexy by leaning up against the front door in a relaxed, tongue-hanging-out-of-my-mouth sort of a way, when the door opens and I'm hurled across the threshold on to the feet of Miss Ballantyne.

73

"Where's Sherene?" I ask. "I've come to pick her up." Miss Ballantyne picks me up instead and gives me a kiss, a big red lipsticky one that sticks to my cheek like tomato sauce and blends with my blushes.

"Who's Sherene?" she laughs, shining my bald head with a yellow duster. "You're my little ballet dancer, you handsome little man." And with that she turns back inside and beckons me forward, just as Miss Purple Uniform pulls up on her bike and starts laughing at me. A cruel, mocking laugh as she points at my legs. And Alison's crying and pointing down there too.

"How could you do this to me, Johnny?" she weeps. "When you know how much I love you!" And I try to explain that I didn't know I was wearing frilly pink tights and a tutu, but she gets the hump and walks away.

Then Ginger pops up beside me and says, *"Good riddance, mate. Come and have a kick-around instead."*

"Never!" I yell. "I want Alison back!" Then he points to a busload of girls that has just arrived and every one of their faces is twisted with glee.

"They're laughing at your hairless nut," says Ginger. As if I didn't know that! And Mrs Ballantyne has gone and Mum is standing in her place, looking all smug with her arms crossed.

"You see, Johnny," she gloats. "I told you, pumpkin, but you wouldn't listen. You should have had more cut off!" But that doesn't make sense.

"More cut off!? Like what?" I ask her, patting my shiny scalp. *"My ears?"*

"Good idea," she says, which takes me somewhat by surprise, especially when she leans forward and cuts off my ears with a lobster's claw.

And then I woke up. I was sweating like a race-horse. I felt my hair to check that the scalping had just been a nightmare, but I was in for a big shock. The top of my head was as smooth as a baby's bum. I was as bald as a bowling ball. My sacred hair had gone!

"That'th 'cauthe you've got your pillow over your head," lisped Sherene, who was standing watching me.

"What do you want?" I growled, chucking the pillow at her head.

"Daddy sayth it'th time to get up, becauthe it'th Mummy'th birthday." I'd forgotten to set my alarm. It was a tradition on Mum's birthday that me and Sherene had to stagger downstairs at 6.30 to help Dad cook a surprise breakfast.

"I'll be down in a minute," I groaned. "Now push off!" There was something I had to do first.

My dream had crystallized what I'd suspected all along. Alison did love me. She did want me to ask her out on a date. I'd just misinterpreted her body language, that was all. What I'd been reading as rejection was obviously seduction. She was playing hard to get. Love's a funny old stick, the way it creeps up behind you and bashes your brains in when you're least expecting it. I thought I'd got Alison out of my system when I'd chucked her last night in favour of Purple, but obviously not. Her sultry beauty still bewitched me. So why was I making love to Purple when my heart lay bleeding elsewhere? Alison was the one. She'd told me herself in the middle of the night. I tore open the pink envelope and removed Purple's love poem.

True luv does never end sometimes.

It seemed a shame to waste such sweet words and, if I was clever, Alison would never know I'd written them for another girl first. I tippexed out the words "To My Purple Goddess" and printed Alison's initials over the top in red felt-tip pen. Unfortunately most of the ink slipped off the shiny coating of Tippex rendering the letters invisible, and the ink that trickled over the edge of the white correcting blob spiked out across the rough paper like streaks of red lightning. By the time I'd finished going over and over the A and the M, they looked like two red Christmas trees, but I didn't have time to do the whole thing again, because Dad was yelling at me to come downstairs and be a useful member of the family for once. So I sealed the card in a second pink envelope, popped it into my blazer pocket, pulled on my school uniform and raced down to the kitchen.

ON KISSING ALISON

Soggy wet lips
with cold saliva on.
Soggy wet cheeks
All running with goo.
Soggy wet teeth
It sounds disgusting,
BUT,
If I have to have a kiss,
I hope it's with you.

(Johnny Casanova — the gigolo with the wigolo)

8
HAPPY BIRTHDAY TO MUM

The trouble with Dad is he still thinks I'm a kid. He whipped me out of bed at 6.30 to help do Mum's surprise breakfast and then didn't trust me to touch a thing in case I did it wrong! He insisted on doing everything himself. He boiled the kettle, sliced the toast, even laid the table, while Sherene and I drooped around like wet tea towels. He has this special system for laying tables, you see, which only he can understand. He uses a template that he's cut out of an old carboard box, with holes in appropriate places for all the utensils. Napkin far left, on the left of the fork at ninety degrees to the scoop of the spoon, running horizontally across the plate with the crest at the top to the tip of the knife lying parallel to the plate on the right hand side, to the left of the cup with the handle to the right, and the teaspoon stuck in the middle. We did offer to help, but

Dad just laughed, informing us that this was no job for children, this was real man's work. Real bore's work, Uncle Stan called it. I wanted to agree with him, but I was only Dad's son, whereas Uncle Stan was Dad's brother so he could say what he liked.

"I came early," grinned Uncle Stan when Dad glowered at him, "to wish the old girl many happies. But now I'm here I might as well have some brekker. Who's cooking?"

"I am," said Dad.

"Oh dear," frowned Uncle Stan. "Then, perhaps I won't stay, after all!" This was an old joke, but Uncle Stan still found it funny. He rocked backwards and forwards on the kitchen chair, sucking in great gulps of air to feed his sonic boom of a laugh.

"Stop rocking that chair or you'll break it," said Dad, who didn't like being made fun of by his younger brother.

"I could have spent another half an hour in bed," I said. This annoyed Dad even more, but not half as much as when Uncle Stan picked up his knife and fork and pretended he was a lorry driver, by banging them on the table and calling for "double bubble and mash". Anyway, this was how Mum found us when she eventually came down: Dad cursing the grill for burning the toast, and me, Sherene and Uncle Stan sitting round the table picking our teeth.

* * *

"Scrumdumtious!" lied Mum, as she crunched her way through her third piece of crispy charcoal. "Thank you, pumpkins. I must be the luckiest little woman in the whole wide world!"

"Open my card firtht!" shouted Sherene, flopping her hand-drawn offering in front of Mum's face. Mum pretended to be surprised.

"Oh, Sherene," she cooed. "Isn't that lovely? Look at what Sherene's done for me, Stanley. It's lovely, isn't it?" She held Sherene's card up so that everyone could see it.

"What is it?" grouched Dad, who'd lost his sense of humour.

"Oh, Daddy!" chided Mum, stroking Sherene's curly head. "Honestly, you men! It's a carrot with a little mouse nibbling at it, isn't it, Sherene?"

"It'th not a cawwot, at all. It'th a houthe!" shrieked Sherene, indignantly.

"Oh yes," said Mum, quickly turning the card the right way up. "It's a pretty, little house. Isn't that clever, Stanley? She's a regular little Picarse-o, aren't you, Sherene?" But Sherene was sulking again.

"Appawently, I can't even dwaw houtheth now!" she grumbled, kicking me under the table. I'd have kicked her back if it hadn't been Mum's birthday. Instead, I generously told Dad to go next, savouring the knowledge that

80

I had a rather special, plastic brooch in my pocket. I wanted to save my present till last, so that I could have Mum's undivided adoration all to myself. Dad produced a small box from behind the microwave and slid it across the table. We all watched as she opened it. Her hands were quivering with excitement and she couldn't get her fingernails under the sellotape.

"Ooh, what is it?" she giggled. "I bet it's earrings, Terry. Is it earrings? Or a little pearl necklace?"

"It's a packet of nicotine chewing gum," said Dad. And it was too. Mum's face fell about three and a half miles.

"Oh, Terry," she said, tersely. "You shouldn't have." And she meant it.

"It's to stop you smoking when you cook my breakfast," said Dad. "I thought you'd like it." I'm not so sure Mum did. Her mouth went all tight and pinched, but it softened and opened up like a flower when Uncle Stan produced a gift-wrapped box from underneath the table.

"It's from Bond Street," he said proudly. "So don't say I never spoil you!" It was extraordinary watching Mum's reaction. She went all coy and girly, and kept glancing up at Uncle Stan while she was opening it. And when she saw what he'd given her she took leave of her senses.

"Ooooooh, it's lovely!" she screeched, taking an antique silver brooch, inset with sparkling diamonds, out of the box. "Oh, Stanley, it's the nicest little present I've ever had!"

I sat there feeling my whole world had come to an end. If I gave Mum my plastic brooch now, it'd be like parking a Skoda next to a Porsche. But there was worse to come. I watched in amazement as Mum leapt up from the table, flung her arms around Uncle Stan's neck, and kissed him all over his face.

"Oh, yeuch!" shrieked Sherene. "Thtop it! It'th embawwathing!"

"I love you, Stan, I do! You're a gorgeous, lovely, hunk of a man!" And Mum kissed him again, several hundred times in several hundred different little places. Dad coughed loudly, like he had some small, furry forest creature wedged in the back of his throat.

"Johnny!" he said, desperate to move the celebration on. "Come on, it's your turn." But I was paralysed by the sudden realization that jewellery was the key to a woman's heart. I only had to look at my over-excited Mum gushing like a giggly schoolgirl on Uncle Stan's lap to see that. I couldn't waste the only brooch I'd got on *her*! I didn't want Mum's kisses, I wanted Alison's. "Johnny!" My dad was sounding cross now. "What have you got your mother?" It was make or break time. I had to think fast.

82

"Hello," I stalled. "Here I am."

"Your mother's present," roared my dad. He was heading for another bad day.

"Shouldn't Pongo give his present first?"

"Pongo doesn't give presents," snapped my dad. "He's a dog." But Pongo thought it most unfair that he should be excluded from the present-giving and, on hearing his name called, thumped his tail on the floor and drifted a personalized greeting across the kitchen table. He was banished into the garden to turn the grass brown, but his whiffle had given me time to think.

"My present. Yes ... er ... you see, the thing is, Mum," I simpered, fluttering my long eyelashes at her, "I haven't got you one." Dad flew up out of his chair like a grizzly bear that'd sat on a cactus.

"You what?" he growled. The inside of his glasses had steamed up.

"Oh, sit down, Terry," said Mum, sharply. "I don't mind."

"I mean, I have," I lied. "Only it's not a present. I mean, I've written you a poem, instead." I'd remembered the pink envelope inside my blazer pocket in the nick of time. "Happy Birthday, Mum!" Her face melted into marshmallow bliss.

"Oh, aren't you sweet, pumpkin! Is it a love poem to your dear old mum?" She was teasing me.

"Sort of," I blushed. I couldn't tell her it was a love letter to Alison Mallinson, could I?

"True luv does never end sometimes," she read, wiping a tear from the corner of her eye. "Isn't that lovely? I love you too, Johnny." And she gave me a great, big slimy wet one on the cheek. "Only what does A.M. stand for? It says here A.M., look."

"A.M.?" I'd forgotten that. "A.M.? Yes … well spotted. Erm … A.M. stands for … erm … well, you'll notice that there's a J. Casanova there as well, Mum, and so that's standing for Jiovanni Casanova loves A.M., which means that the M is obviously for … erm … Mummy, and the A is for…" I couldn't think what it was for. "Erm … A is for…"

"Alithon?" suggested Sherene.

"Shut up, will you? No, A is for … Ant." Mum was confused.

"Jiovanni Casanova loves Ant Mummy?" She wasn't the only one.

"Yes," I bluffed, "A.N.T. Short for A Nice Terrific. A Nice Terrific Mummy. There!"

"Oh," said Mum. "Well, I think that's lovely."

"I thtill think it'th Alithon," said Sherene. I'd get her later.

"No, you see, you said yesterday that what you'd really love for your birthday was Jiovanni Casanova, so I thought I'd give him to you."

"What?" roared my dad. Mum kicked me under the table.

"Oh, look," she giggled nervously, "you've spelt Giovanni with a J not a G, it must be his brother." She was whinnying now like a nervous horse. "Isn't that super!" My dad had got out of his chair again.

"So you want an Italian gigolo for your birthday, do you? Faithful old Terry suddenly not good enough for you, eh?"

"Don't be silly," smiled Mum, flicking her hair out of her eyes. "'Course you are, pumpkin." Then she hissed under her breath, "Not in front of the children!" and carried on laughing, only it was a strange laugh. It came out of her mouth all right and she looked like she meant it, but her eyes were flashing fury and weren't laughing at all.

Fortunately, that was when the doorbell rang and gave me an excuse to leave the room. Unfortunately, it was Ginger on his bike, seeing if I was ready for school. I nearly died when I opened the door and saw him standing there, because I knew that somehow I'd have to tell him I'd fallen back in love with Alison, and when I did he'd call me a two-faced dipstick and stop being my best friend. I decided I couldn't do it there and then. I'd wait till I was in a big open space, so that if Ginger fainted he wouldn't hit his head, and if he tried to bash my brains in I could run away.

"Hello, Ginger," purred Sherene's voice. My simpering sister had sneaked under my arm and was rubbing up against the door jamb like a pleasure-seeking cat. "I thought it wath you." Ginger's face flushed scarlet as Sherene's hero-worshipping eyes ate him alive. "Have I ever told you that I think you're more handthomer than Johnny?"

"Shut up," I said. "You're embarrassing him."

"Well, he ith, tho there!" stamped Sherene, sticking her tongue out at me. Ginger had backed off as far as the front gate.

"Hurry up!" he winced, but Sherene hadn't finished with him yet.

"You know thomething, Ginger," she shouted for all the neighbours to hear. "I think you're a PLP." Ginger wasn't naturally comfortable with this game.

"What's a PLP?" he muttered, trying to lower the volume of their conversation.

"NO!" screamed Sherene. "You're meant to thay, 'What, you mean I'm a Public Leaning Potht?'"

"Do I have to?" pleaded Ginger.

"Yeth!" barked his persecutor. He checked up and down the road for passers-by and took a deep breath.

"What, you mean I'm a Public Leaning Post?" he squirmed. Sherene giggled at the clever trick she had just played on him.

"No," she swooned, "I think you're a Perfectly Lovely Perthon!"

"JOHNNY! WILL YOU HURRY UP!" screamed the scruffy object of Sherene's desire. Ginger was eager to go.

While this nauseating billing and cooing was going on, I slipped back into the empty kitchen to get my school bag. Mum and Dad had gone into the garden to continue their row, Uncle Stan had escaped into the loo to make himself invisible and there, lying right in the middle of the table where Mum had dropped it, was the silver brooch, radiating temptation. I couldn't take my eyes off it. I mean, was it really right to give my beloved Alison a piece of plastic jewellery that I knew was a worthless scrap of old toot, when I could be giving her the real thing, something of lasting value, something expensive and flashy to prove that I treasured her – namely, this diamond-studded brooch? And if I did take it, I'd only be borrowing it until Alison gave me a kiss, then I'd ask for it back. Besides, by the black look on Dad's face when Uncle Stan had given it to Mum, I reckoned I'd be doing the family a favour by getting the silver brooch out of the house for a while.

Before anyone could come in, I sneaked it into my blazer pocket and substituted Mr

Patel's cheap bit of plastic nonsense with fake gems in. They'd never notice. Then I grabbed my bike from the lean-to and joined Ginger in the street, where he was keener than I'd seen him in a long while to set off for that Sherene-free zone known as school.

ON PARENTS AND POSSESSIONS

Dad's got a gnome called Norman
Hunter.
Dad's got a gnome called Fred
Astaire.
Dad's got a gnome called Rory
Underwood.
I don't think Dad's all there.

Mum's got a brooch with diamond
studs on.
Mum's got a brooch with a silver pin.
Mum's also got a brooch which is
made out of plastic,
And when Mum finds out
She's going to do me in.

(Anon — because I don't want Mum to
know it was me who took it)

9
COURTING DISASTER

I'd decided to give Mum's brooch to Alison during the lunchbreak, which meant I didn't learn diddly-squit that morning. Waves of manly lust kept mugging my mind and sending my body into spasms of desire. By the time the lunch bell rang, I was hotter than a baby-oiled Chippendale. I felt like the Incredible Hulk splitting his shirt down the back, as I exploded into manhood with rippling biceps and sledgehammer thighs.

"Are you all right?" queried my science teacher as I left the lab.

"I'm a living sex machine," I replied, much to her surprise.

Alison was sitting alone on her favourite bench in the corner of the playground. Timothy was off singing in the school choir in some church or other in Hackney so I had her all to myself. As I didn't want Ginger finding out what I was up to – he'd only make a scene in front of Alison and call me a liar and a plonker while I was trying to do the business – I skirted round the playground fence, using the trees as cover and appeared as if by magic behind Alison's slender shoulders. It was now or never. I licked my lips, sucked in my cheeks and was just about to go in for the kill when a female flying bomb gutbusted me from behind.

"Yesterday you called me De-BORE-ah, you gorgeous hunk!" trembled the metallic lump on top of me.

"This is not a good time," I choked, wrenching Deborah's hands from around my neck and pushing myself up on to my forearms. She slipped off my back like half a hundredweight of builder's sand sliding off a dump-truck. I stood up, but Deborah threw her arms around my legs. "What are you doing?" I exclaimed.

"You've made me the happiest girl in the world," she flushed, hugging on to my knees. I tried to pull away, but she had a tight grip. "I want to marry you and have your babies!" Alison turned round to see what the noise was and looked straight at me.

"Oh, hi!" I waved, trying to look cool by pretending that Deborah wasn't there, but she was squeezing my knees together and I crashed to the ground like a one-legged giraffe. Alison stood up and moved away to the next bench. If I didn't act fast, I'd lose her.

"I don't love you, Debra," I snapped as cruelly as I could. "Now leave me alone. You're pulling the creases out of my trousers!"

"De-BORE-ah!" she hissed. "And keep your voice down. I've told everyone that we're engaged, and engaged people are meant to be nice to each other."

"But we're not engaged, Debra. We never have been!"

"It's De-BORE-ah!" she wailed, extending her fingers and grasping hold of my belt.

"And let go of my legs. You're squeezing them out of the bottom of my trousers like toothpaste."

"Not until you say you love me!" she demanded. I stood up and tried to walk away, but she clung on and dragged behind me like a lead-lined wedding veil.

"Cecil," I cried. "Cecil, help!"

"Hello, do you like me?" asked Cecil, who skipped up and waved at Deborah. "Hello, Debra, can I come home with you?"

"De-BORE-ah actually!" she fumed, thumping the deck with her fists and inadvertently releasing me.

"That's what I said," chirruped Cecil. "Do you like me?" I wasted no time in thrusting the two lovebirds together. I sat Cecil down on top of Deborah and told him not to move until the

91

end of break or else Deborah wouldn't love him, but just as I got away from my metal-mouthed Harpy, who should butt in but Ginger.

"What's going on?" he said.

"Nothing," I replied casually, hoping he'd believe me and go and play football. I couldn't ask Alison out for a date with Ginger there.

"So what was all the shouting for?"

"Debra was trying to get my trousers off!" I laughed, trying to joke my way out of the situation, but Hell hath no fury like a woman scorned!

"He was trying to see Alison," said Deborah, swiftly spiking my lie.

"I thought I told you to sit on her, Cecil," I barked.

"You did," said Cecil, "but she bit my bottom with her metal teeth. Do you still like me?" Ginger's face had turned a vivid shade of purple.

"So that's why you've been avoiding me," he seethed. "You're after Alison again."

"No," I lied. "You've got it all wrong."

"I thought you loved the purple girl. That's what you said last night."

"Ah, yes... Purple. Well, you see, there's been a tiny change of plan, Ginge, old mate," I said, sheepishly. "Love moves in a mysterious way."

"So will you if Timothy ever gets hold of

92

you. I give up on you, Johnny."

"No, you don't understand. This time it's meant to be," I said, "because I've had a sign. A bit like Mary had before she popped Jesus."

"What are you talking about?"

"In a dream," I explained.

"You saw an angel?"

"Well, sort of... I saw a vision of loveliness. Alison came to me in my dream and said we had a date." Ginger threw his hands in the air and fixed me with a stare of profound disappointment.

"Let us know when you're ready to be best friends again," he said and, with that, he just walked away, which should have been a problem, but as it happens didn't affect me one bit, because it left Alison and me with a bit of privacy.

I slipped on to the seat beside her and casually draped my arm across the back of the bench, walking my fingers slowly along the wooden path towards her neck.

"Go away," she said, without even looking at me. "I don't like you one little bit, Johnny Worms, or hadn't you noticed?"

"The name's Johnny Casanova!" I said, expecting fireworks to go off inside her head, but the blue touch paper must've been damp.

"You are the most boring person in the world," she informed me. "If I had a choice between walking out with you, or kissing a nearly-dead, slimy-green, wart-ridden slug with a head cold, I'd choose the slug every time!" I laughed at her lover's tease.

"I take it you do love me then?" I said.

"You are an insufferable little oik!" she raged, tossing her hair out of her eyes and standing up sharply. "I wish you'd go away and die somewhere, horribly!" This was not promising, but I played the old courting trick of calling her bluff.

"Sure," I said. "Sure thing, but it means you won't get your present." I started to move away, expecting Alison to stop me. But she didn't. "I said, I've bought you a very expensive present, but if you don't want it, well..." There was still no response. "I'll keep it." Alison closed her eyes to signify that she was not listening. "Well, don't you even want to know what it is?"

"No." The two-letter word sprang off her tongue like an arched scorpion.

"It's a diamond brooch," I said. "It's a token of my love." The scent of victory in my nostrils, I produced Mum's birthday present and pressed it into Alison's hand. "For you," I said, half closing my eyes in anticipation of the shower of kisses she was going to give me when she clocked how generous I'd been. I waited for the touch of her soft lips; and waited ... and waited ... and waited... And when I opened my eyes Alison was walking away. Love struck, I thought, definitely a serious case of lovestruckness. Her head's in a whirl, she doesn't know where she is, poor petal. I went after her. "There is one other thing," I panted, while she kept walking. "I want a date tonight. That's what the brooch is for." Alison's patent leathers trudged on, but I persisted. "Shall I take that as a yes, then?"

"Oh look," she said, stopping suddenly. "There's Debra Smeeton. I've been meaning to have a chat with her." She turned and looked me straight in the eye. "All right, Johnny, I will go out on a date with you. After all, it is a very lovely brooch." She slid it into her breast pocket. "Come to my house at seven o'clock tonight. Number 35 Munster Mews. And, Johnny…"

"Yes," I simpered.

"Don't be late!" Then she smiled at me in a sly, crooked sort of way and crossed the playground to talk to Deborah. I couldn't believe it. She'd said yes! I stood there gawping at her, like a bemused man who'd just watched a pile of manure turn into gold. Then I clutched my arms across my chest and spun round on the spot, making the clouds whirl above my head. I was going out with Alison Mallinson!

After school, I cycled home on an air cushion of bliss. I had a self-satisfied grin plastered to my face, which gave me a well-crumpled but gently appealing look – a bit like Pongo's. My head was all in a passionate fug about Alison, full of lush romantic thoughts as a thousand pink cupids played postman's knock through the letterboxes of my mind. It came as something of a shock, therefore, when I turned into Nelson's Way and eyeballed a purple blazer and a pair of baggy black tights.

I'd clean forgotten about Purple, and now here she was cycling towards me and presenting me with something of a dilemma. Now that I was somebody else's boyfriend what was I meant to do? Ignore her or engage her in pleasant conversation? I mean, was I being unfaithful just chatting? Was I ratting on Alison if I took one tiny peek? Surely not. Besides, Purple's gorgeous blonde hair was trailing behind her like a trawler's drag net and raising goosebumps on the tips of my vertebrae. Oh, that sensual Siren! It'd be a crying shame if I never actually tried out my cunning bike crash ploy on her. I mean, what if things didn't work out with Alison? I'd be crazy not to have a girlfriend in reserve. She was coming closer. Should I? Yes! Go on! Crash-time! Now! What was a moment of pain compared to a night at the Streatham Ritzy? Courage, Casanova! I felt the love drug rushing through my system like a fireball, sparking me with dash and fervour, razing self doubt to the ground. She was right alongside me. I could smell her sweet I-had-steak-and-kidney-pie-for-lunch breath. Jump, you fool, jump! But my bottom was stuck to the saddle like a velcroed peach. My lips had once again sealed up like a self-sticking envelope and she glided past without so much as a glance in my direction. I was watching her disappear down the road when my front wheel hit the kerb and I was thrown fifteen feet in the air, spinning back to earth with a splash. It was total humiliation, sitting there in the shallows of the ornamental duck pond, with bindweed round my ears, mud lapping over my shoes and a toad sitting plumb in the middle of my forehead.

ODE TO TOADS

Toads is warty,
Toads ooze slime,
Toads is ugly
All the time.
So,
What is it that a toad possesses,
That brings it kisses from princesses?
I'm a boy with luvly hair,
They should kiss ME!
It just ain't fair!

(Johnny Casanova is 007 — Licensed to kiss)

10
PREPARATIONS FOR THE ALTAR OF LOVE

When I got home I jumped straight in the bath. Mum and Dad weren't around to dispense love and sympathy, so a tank of warm water seemed the next best thing for thawing cold bones. I poured in half a bottle of banana bubble bath and sank into the fruity froth till it filled up my ears. The next thing I knew I was being woken up by Pongo dribbling on my face. The bathroom door was wide open and a cold draught whipped across the icy water like a polar wind. My fingers and toes had wrinkled like prunes and my body was bright blue.

"What's the time?" I groaned, as Pongo salivated down my neck. "What is it? What do you want?" He was trying to warn me of something. I could tell by the way he was nuzzling his cold, tickling snout into my armpit. "Do you mind?" I protested feebly, but Pongo just wagged his tail and nuzzled some more. "Oh, all right, I'm listening." Whereupon my decrepit pet whimpered and looked as sad as he possibly could, which wasn't difficult for a bloodhound. "There's a problem?" I guessed. Pongo wagged his tail vigorously, like he was congratulating me for being so clever. "All right," I sighed. "So, how bad is this problem, exactly?" I watched through bleary eyes as Pongo puzzled this one out. How was he going to express degrees of awfulness without the power of speech? He couldn't draw pictures, he couldn't write it down, he couldn't... Ah! He lifted his tail. My face turned inside out as his flatulent fall-out singed the hairs in my nostrils. "That bad, eh?" I choked, as Pongo shook his head and lifted his tail for a second time. "Oh, THAT bad!" I retched, as the old dog re-established his ranking as World Number One Ozone Layer Destroyer. "Yeah, thanks, Pongo, I don't think we need any more demonstrations, actually." Pongo sat down in a job-well-done sort of a way and watched me turn a vivid shade of green.

"Pongo'th wight," said a squeaky voice from the door. Sherene had crept upstairs to see if I was dead.

"Look, I'm having a bath!" I complained, using Mum's flannel to cover my shrivelled winkle. "Get out!" But Sherene wasn't going anywhere till she'd told me the news.

"Thingth are a little bit whoopth-keep-your-head-down-if-you-don't-wantth-it-mathed-up-like-a-yucky-thwede awound here, at the moment!"

"Why?" I asked.

"Becauthe," replied Sherene in her bored, if-I-have-to-tell-another-person-this-story-I'm-going-to-kill-them voice, "becauthe Mummy'th lotht her diamond bwooch. I think Pongo'th eaten it. I thuggethted we put him on the kitchen table and cut him open, but Mummy told me to athk Daddy and Daddy told me to athk Mummy and Mummy told me to go away, tho that'th that weally." I sat up quickly.

"Oh," I said. "Mum's brooch."

"You know where it ith, don't you?" said Sherene, accusingly.

"No, I don't," I lied.

"Well, if you do, I withh you'd tell her, 'cauthe thhe'th charging awound downth-tairth like a vewy angwy dwagon indeed. Look what thhe did to me!" She shoved her head into my face. Her hair was sticking up in wet clumps and smelt like it'd been washed in bath cleaner. The sharp stench made me jerk backwards and crack my head against the enamel.

"What on earth is that?" I bleurghed.

"I've got nitth," said Sherene. "It doethn't mean I'm dirty, but it doeth mean I've got to have thith yucky thtuff, what thtinkth the roof

off, on my head, and you're next, tho there!"
I pushed her away before she suffocated me,
just as Mum burst into the room and joined
Sherene by the side of my bath.

"Do you mind?" I shouted. "Can't a man
get any privacy around here? If I'd known
you all wanted to look, I'd have sold tickets!"
But I'd chosen the wrong moment to make my
protest. Mum was steaming. The veins in her
forehead were pumping blood like firemen's
hoses, her platinum blonde hair had burst
from its grips and was hanging down over her
eyes like a manky mop.

"Brooch!" she hissed. "Brooch!" Dad
arrived at a run behind her.

"It's all right, love. We'll find it!" He tried
to restrain her, but she just shook him off and
grabbed hold of my flannel.

"Brooch!" she grunted again, whipping it
off my legs and peering underneath for her
precious jewel. "Brooch?"

"No. Willy," I said furiously, but she was
stuck in a groove.

"Brooch!" she moaned. "Brooch!" Dad led
her out of the room. "Brooch!"

"How about a nice stiff drink and a couple
of sleeping pills?" he offered, tenderly. Then,
just as he was about to close the door he leaned
back into the room and said, "She's lost her
brooch. Either that or the silver's turned to
plastic." He threw Mr Patel's junk copy into

101

the waste paper bin. "See if you can't find the real one, son. Only we're going posh for her birthday at the Harvester and she's quite keen to wear it."

"Sure thing," I smiled, but I didn't need to look, because I knew where it was already. Snuggling down where I longed to be; inside Alison Mallinson's breast pocket! "Oh, my God!" I leapt out of the bath, bundled Sherene to one side and grabbed a towel. "Alison Mallinson! What's the time?" For all I knew, I'd missed our date. Sherene consulted her new wrist watch.

"Well," she said slowly, "the big hand'th on the thix, and the little hand'th on the..."

"Come on," I shouted, grabbing her wrist.

"I than't tell you if you thnatch," she said, wrenching her arm free. "The little hand'th on the... It'th vewy hard thith time-telling thing, ithn't it?"

"No," I screamed. "The little hand's on the what?"

"The thix too," she announced.

"Six thirty!" I wailed. "Six pigging thirty! Why didn't you wake me earlier? I'm meant to be there in half an hour and I still haven't done my hair!"

"Or ith it the five?" puzzled Sherene. "Yeth, it'th the five, which maketh it..."

"Five thirty," I yelped. "I could kill you sometimes."

"Weally?" said my dopey little sister. "Would you kill me for a million poundth or jutht ten?"

"For free," I snapped, chucking her out of the bathroom. Then I locked the door and set about rescuing my sacred hair.

The plan was this. After I'd had a snog with Alison, I'd get the brooch back and sneak it under Mum's pillow, as if the fairies had left it there or something, then everything would be back to normal. I flattened a stubborn curl across my forehead with a practised flick of cold water. The only other problem was where to take the girl. I tore a piece of loo paper off the roll and used Mum's lipstick to write down a list of possible venues.

1) OYSTER BAR: This was a great idea and one that I'd been longing to try out for ages, ever since I'd heard that oysters made girls sexy, but then I remembered that I'd seen someone eating an oyster in a restaurant last year and it had looked like snot, so I went off this idea fast.

2) CHAMPAGNE BALLOON FLIGHT: Now I was cooking. A ride to the stars in our own private love basket. What could be more romantic? Trouble was, I hadn't done anything about booking a flight, I didn't like heights and champagne made me bugle, so I gave this one the elbow too.

3) HARRODS' TOY DEPARTMENT: A quirky date, but I'd read somewhere that girls liked surprises, and spending the evening racing model rally cars round a fifty-foot Scalextric track would certainly surprise Alison. But what if I won (because I would) and what if Harrods was closed (which it would be)? Harrods bit the dust too.

Selecting the perfect date was a lot harder than I'd imagined. It was easy going out with Ginger, because we liked the same things; hamburgers, films and more hamburgers, but Alison's tastes were unknown to me. It was like trying to come up with a list of places that might appeal to a Paraguayan Chinchilla.

4) LATE NIGHT SHOPPING: Girls liked shopping. But I didn't. So that was that one down the pan.

5) THE GARDEN CENTRE: I could show her where Dad bought his gnomes.

I was getting desperate.

6) THE OPERA: What did she think I was? Made of money?

7) THE CINEMA: Yes! The cinema was inspired. Dark enough so she wouldn't see my hand sneaking round her shoulder and loud enough to cover her scream when she did. And it was cheap. I re-inspected my sacred thatch from all sides and scuttled out of the bathroom, taking great care to check that my mad Mum wasn't lurking inside the airing cupboard.

Back in my bedroom, I took my Aston Martin piggy-bank down off the shelf and pressed the exhaust pipe to open up the roof. Then I squeezed my little finger between the seats and the dashboard, and slipped the gear lever into first, unlocking the car's boot. My money was hidden underneath the spare wheel. I spread it out on my bed and counted it. All seven pence! There was nothing else for it; Sherene would have to lend me some. I sneaked into her room and tiptoed out with eleven pounds eighty-three. She'd never miss it, and besides I'd be doing her a favour by spending it on something worthwhile for a change, instead of some stupid, sequinned dress for her Barbie doll. I had six pounds for two tickets and a fiver left over for popcorn. Brill! The flicks it was!

It was 6.15. I had fifteen minutes left before I had to go, fifteen crucial minutes in which to choose some mega-heavy gear to impress Alison. I pulled everything out of my wardrobe and scattered it over the floor. I chose my baggiest jeans (the ones that Mum refused to let me wear in public even though she'd bought them for me), my baggiest T-shirt, which had a picture printed on it of a man sitting on the bog saying "Don't Let The Bastards Grind You Down", my baggiest shirt to go over the top and my Black Jacks, which weren't baggy at all, but then they weren't meant to be. They had huge great workmen's soles, like tractor tyres, and stiff, intractable leather uppers that came to just below my knees and gave me blisters when I walked, but that wasn't the point. I looked cool enough to freeze a chicken.

As I set about the arduous task of lacing up my boots, I heard a thump, thump, thump coming down from the attic. I peered through the keyhole and saw Dad laying a trail of chocolate raisins down the loft ladder. Nan was being coaxed out of her cell to babysit. She passed my door on all fours, hoovering up the raisins like an anteater, and slid over the top step of the staircase like a ski jumper at the top of an icy take-off ramp. I heard the crunch as she landed in the hallway, followed swiftly by Dad's voice.

"Johnny, we're going out now! Look after your grandmother and don't let your sister go to bed too late." I could hear Mum weeping, then the front door clicked and I knew they were gone.

I stood up and asked Pongo how I looked. He thumped his tail and squeaked a rear-ender in my face. I might have known it. Then I kissed my bedroom mirror and lingered a while to savour the imaginary lips of Alison Mallinson. If I closed my eyes and fluttered my eyelashes at triple speed, I could convince myself that my reflection was hers.

TWO HALFS OF A WHOLE

In the mirror, I does see
A lady looking back at me.
She is a doll, most wondrous fair
with ears a nose a mouth and hair.
Her eyes are like two shining golf balls
Her luvly hair, like flowing water
falls.
In the mirror, I does see
My heart in its duplicity.
In the mirror, I does see
Both two of us, that's Alison and me.

(Johnny Casanova — in misty mirror
mode)

When I'd finished fluttering, I ran through final checks before take off, just in case there were any bits of me that weren't quite baggy enough. There weren't.

I took the stairs at a run, sliding down the bannisters on my bottom, and only just avoiding a painful collision with the newel post. I asked Sherene what she thought of my get-up.

"I think your twoutherth are too baggy," she responded, frankly. I was stung.

"Yeah, well, you look like a baby!" I said viciously, striding into the kitchen where Nan was preparing supper. I had five minutes before I had to leave.

"Ready in ten minutes," Nan said. "Johnny, you lay the table. Sherene, you go outside and hose down the sheep's stomach on the washing line." I didn't have time to hang around to see what demonic dish Nan was planning to poison us with. As Sherene dutifully went outside to sluice down the tripe, I clutched my stomach and mumbled my excuses.

"Sorry," I said, backing out of the kitchen, "but I've got to go to the loo."

"Better out than in," Nan said. "Better out than all over the floor!" She cackled at her little joke and I humoured her by joining in.

"I won't be a sec," I lied.

"Don't worry," she said. "We won't start without you." That was the worst news I'd heard all day.

"No, do. Please."

"I wouldn't dream of it, dear. Now off you go to the little boys' room!" And off I went. I wanted Nan to think that I was going upstairs, so I did thirty seconds of loud running-on-the-spot at the bottom of the staircase, before tip-toeing quietly across the hall and stealing one final admire in the sunburst mirror. There was no question about it – I was an unexploded teenage sex bomb. Johnny Casanova – the unstoppable sex machine. Johnny Casanova – one hundred percent pure, muscle-bound beef,

just hoofing the ground to give Alison the time
of her pretty young life!

Then I slipped out through my own front
door like a burglar.

ON BEING NERVOUS FOR MY FIRST DATE

A girl expects what on her first date?
To kiss and cuddle with her mate,
Or sit and chat upon a bench,
Discussing literature and French?
Or does she want a little romance,
Flowers and chocs, a barnyard ho
dance?
Or p'raps she's into politicians,
Scientists and mathematicians,
About which I know plainly zero.
Or maybe I should play the hero,
Leaping over trains and buses,
With the minimum of fusses,
And lay my coat across a puddle.
It really is a dreadful muddle.
Or maybe I should just be me?
Now there's a thought — just plain J.C.
But if I do, and here's the bind,
She might not like what she do find.

(Johnny Casanova — on root to
becoming a grown-up)

11
MY FIRST DATE

Munster Mews was about about ten minutes' walk away on the edge of the common. I'd always imagined that Alison lived in one of those rich mansions with a garage on the side and a row of Christmas trees in the front drive, so I was slightly surprised to find that the houses in Munster Mews were like shoeboxes. Two-up two-down, stone clad dwellings with metal windows, aluminium front doors and rusty prams in their front gardens.

I could have caught a bus to get there, but I wanted to save what little money I had to make a big impression and, besides, you can't get a free bunch of flowers on the top deck of a bus. Front gardens, however, are perfect. By the time I reached Alison's road, I'd helped myself to a huge armful of other peoples' blooms. There were roses, hydrangeas, a few bits of trailing ivy, a small branch off a crabapple tree and a pot of mint that someone had left out in their porch. I was carrying more flowers than a coffin at a State funeral.

I stopped twenty yards down the road from Alison's house and hid behind a pot-bellied laurel bush that was sticking out across the pavement. I didn't want Alison to see me till the last minute, just in case she got cold feet and changed her mind. I checked my watch to see how I was doing timewise. I didn't want to be too early, in case she thought I was over keen. On the other hand, I didn't want to be too late, in case she thought I didn't care. Mind you, I had heard that some girls preferred their boyfriends to turn up late, as they liked to walk out with wild cards and budding Bohemians, and blokes with no sense of time were more interesting than punctual prats who lived life by the clock and never did anything they hadn't planned six weeks in advance. Not that blokes who turned up early couldn't be wild too. They might be wildly in love, which was why they couldn't stay away. I was gored on the twin horns of a dating dilemma. It seemed to me that turning up at any time was likely to lead to trouble, so perhaps I just shouldn't turn up at all. But that was stupid, after all I had just walked a mile across town and I was carrying half of Kew Gardens in my arms.

As I took the plunge and stepped out from

behind the bush, my stomach jittered with nerves. Forget butterflies, I had two hundred bats swooping and chattering inside my bowels and rivulets of cold sweat poured down the inside of my arms like glacial streams. I realized with horror that I'd forgotten to put Dad's deodorant on. So there I was sniffing my armpits, when a lady from the Salvation Army walked by and gave me a really funny look, like I was a New Age Traveller or something. I pretended I was rubbing an itch on my nose with the underside of my bicep and muttered "Hayfever!", pointing to the flowers in my other arm. I could tell by the way she narrowed her nostrils and threw her head back that she didn't believe me and thought I was some sort of juvenile delinquent, but that was OK, because it meant that my baggy jeans and Black Jacks were sending out the right signals. Being a rebel was hard to-the-max and, with that in mind, I swaggered up the front path, leaned casually against the porch and rang Alison's doorbell. It was 7 o'clock precisely. I was bang on time.

I held the flowers out in front of me as the front door opened.

"These," I said, going down on one knee and bowing my head, "are for you, Alison."

"De-BORE-ah actually," said the person who had opened the door. My Passion-Pullman came off the rails with a terrifying screech and plunged into Nightmare Valley.

"You!" I gasped. "What are you doing in Alison's house?"

"I live here."

"With Alison?"

"With Mummy and Daddy, actually. This is my house. So where are you taking me?"

"What?" A joke was a joke, but this was getting scary. "No, no. Not you and me, Debra. This isn't right. You're the wrong girl."

"So how come I've got this, then?" she said triumphantly, flashing Mum's silver brooch at me.

"How did you get that?" I squealed. My voice had gone all high-pitched like a piglet sliding down a razor blade.

"Alison said you were too shy to give it to me yourself."

"Alison!" A machete cleaved my heart in twain. My love had betrayed me. Where had I gone wrong? I'd given her jewellery, hadn't I? I'd even stolen some flowers for her (not that she knew that, of course), only to find that she of all people had set me up on a date with little Miss Metalmouth. She'd stitched me up like a kipper and tricked me into consorting in public with this gormless, gangly, grease-spot of a girl! The known universe in all its infinite size is not large enough to contain the toe-tingling embarrassment that I experienced at that precise moment. Johnny Casanova? More like

113

Johnny No Pants! I was ruined. I'd be a laughing stock! Yet the awful truth remained – I still had to get Mum's brooch back.

"Go back inside. You can't stay out here," I said.

"Why?" she asked. "Do you like my new dress?"

"Because it's much too cold for you out here. It's freezing. Brrrrrr!" I pretended to shiver and flapped my jacket around like bat-wings, apparently to keep myself warm. In fact, I was trying to hide her face from nosey passers-by.

"I sewed the rose petals on this dress, all by myself," she announced. "Don't you want to kiss me hello?"

"No!" I blurted, rather too fast to be kind. "I mean, no thanks, not yet." I didn't want to upset her before I'd retrieved the brooch. "Look, can't we go back inside to discuss your dress?"

"Mummy said it was all right for me to kiss you, so long as I took my brace out first. Otherwise I might give you bloodblisters on your tongue!" I screamed silently inside my head. Deborah was gross to-the-most. She had me trapped – she still had me brooch as well.

"Look," I faltered, "don't take this the wrong way or anything, but it's the brooch I want, not you." I could see she had taken it the wrong way, because she clenched both her fists and turned purple.

"But you gave it to me," she said with a hint of hurt in her voice.

"No, I did not, I gave it to Alison."

"She said you'd say that, but it's me you love really. She said so."

"Well, I'm sorry to disappoint you, Debra…"

"De-BORE-ah, actually!"

"De-BORE-ah actually, but I don't. I just want the brooch."

"Well, you can't have it!" she stamped, placing her hand over her lapel to protect her solid silver investment. Somewhere along the line I'd misplayed my hand. There was a tap on the window. A woman with greasy black hair, huge cinemascope glasses that were wider than her face, a long, crimped nose and buck teeth to ski down grinned at us through the glass. "My mother," said Deborah. It had to be really. The Frankenstein family resemblance was frightening. "She's waiting for you to take me out," she explained. "You see, every single one of the boys I've ever gone out with has done what you're trying to do now. Dump me on the doorstep before the date's even started."

"So?" I said.

"So Mummy's promised to put a stop to it." Deborah smiled. "She's watching to see what you do, because in her apron pocket she's got a butcher's knife and if you don't take me out, she's going to slice your ears off like two fig

115

rolls!" It was hard to tell if Deborah was joking or not, but as her Mummy had a grin like a mad axewoman I believed her. "Now, here's what I suggest you do," she said. "One, you stop pretending that you don't love me, because I know that you do. Two, you stand up like a man and take me out like you promised, and three, you make darned sure that whenever I ask you to kiss me, you kiss me, because when you've kissed me, then I might, and I mean only might, return your brooch. OK? Let's go." Then she slapped me hard about the face three times and steered me down the pavement by the seat of my pants. And in that brief moment, as I struggled under the weight of Deborah's thumb, I realized why some men take up golf.

ON A DATE WITH THE DEVIL

There's nothing more undignified
Than being taken for a ride,
Specially when the girl's not nice
And grabs your baggies in a vice,
And hitches them up to the sky,
Bringing tear drops to your eye.

(Johnny Casanova — with a cold hand on my trousers)

Deborah would insist on holding my hand as we walked to the cinema. I tried all sorts of tickling tricks and manual manoeuvres to extricate my fingers, but she clung on for dear life, with a grip as tight as an insecure boa constrictor's. Unable to escape her attentions, I insisted that we took the scenic route to our destination, round the back of the shoe factory, past the kitchens of the Chinese take-away and up through the tiny alleyway that bissected the abattoir and the sewage plant. Invisibility from the public eye was para-mount. If anybody saw me with Deborah, I'd be forced to commit suicide by disembowel-ling myself on a parking meter. I tried not to look at her either. I stared in the opposite direction and pretended that I wasn't with her. Had we been discovered, I was quite prepared to disown her completely by leaping from her clutches (as one might leap away from a tentacled space alien that had suddenly materialized by one's side) and by screaming, "Ugh! Ugh! Ugh! Look what's just grown on the end of my arm! Quick! Someone get a doctor to amputate it!"

We skirted round the back of the Odeon and approached the entrance through the dark shadows of a scaffolding rig. Then we slipped into the foyer through a side door and made base camp inside a public telephone booth. I unscrewed the light bulb from its socket and

117

peered out at the crowd.

"Why are we hiding in here?" enquired Deborah. "Why aren't we out there, buying tickets to see a film?" I was scanning the foyer for familiar faces.

"Don't you always do this when you come to the cinema?" I asked, innocently. "Squash up in a public telephone box while you decide what you want to see?"

"No," said Deborah, "but I must say, I do like the squashing up bit!" She rubbed closer, dragging her shoes across the nylon carpet and sending a blue spark crackling between two spot welds in the bridge of her mouth. Fortunately, the foyer was all clear, so we were able to make a dash for the box office before she set my nose hairs alight.

"What will it be?" I asked, "*Lethal Australian, Eat My Ninja Fist, Robot on the Rampage* or *Howard's Entrails?*"

"But they're all Fifteens and Eighteens," whispered Deborah. "I'm only thirteen."

"Quite right. I should never have brought you here. Let's go," I said quickly, seizing Deborah's arm and spinning her round before she could change her mind. But as we took a step towards the exit, my feet turned to cement inside my Black Jacks. I could move neither forwards into the foyer nor backwards to the box office, for in both directions lay abject humiliation. There on the pavement, wearing denim shorts over her thick black tights, stood my sweet purple object of desire, looking all the sweeter now that Alison had dumped me. The sight of that long blonde hair, tumbling down her back like sun-ripe corn, took hold of my gut and twisted it like a wet towel. So, there I was, good and gooey, hyper-ventilating on the brown swirly carpet in the foyer, while she laughed in the road with another man. I hated him. She pawed at his denim jacket as they came through the door, throwing her long slender arm around his spotty, red, pillar-box neck. It was so unfair. What could she possibly see in him?

"What are you staring at?" It was Deborah. I had forgotten she was there. Alarm bells rang inside my head as I entertained the gruesome possibility that I might have to introduce the two girls. I imagined Deborah's dental harness slipping from her mouth and falling to the floor as she said "Hi". I couldn't let them meet. I couldn't let Miss Perfect-Purple see me here with Miss De-BORE-ah Actually. She'd think we were going steady, and then I'd never get to speak to her, no matter how convincingly I crashed my bike or broke my bones. There was nothing else for it, I would have to buy two tickets and lose Deborah inside one of the dingy corridors that criss-crossed the cinema complex.

"Two for *Lethal Australian*, please," I said.

"It's a fifteen," replied the pear-drop sucking lady behind the cash till.

"What? Oh, I see," I laughed. "You think this girl, MY SISTER..." I dropped that bit in extra loud, in case the Purple Goddess was eavesdropping. "You think my sister isn't fifteen. Well, I can vouch for her, actually." The lady rattled the sweet between her teeth.

"It's not your sister I'm worried about," she said. "It's you." My world disintegrated like a ten pound note in a washing machine.

"I am fifteen," I said. I tried to shove my voice down into my boots, but it broke free and sprang up three octaves. "I've been shaving for years."

"I bet you have," said Deborah. "Don't you think he's gorgeous?" she added, ruffling her fingers through my hair.

"He may be gorgeous," replied the lady, "but he's only ten."

"Ten!" The word exploded out of my mouth, silencing the buzz in the foyer and ensuring that everyone heard what followed. "I'll have you know, I'm thirteen!" And there was my mistake. It was worse than being in one of those anxiety dreams, where you have to stand up in front of the whole class and read your English essay in the buff.

"Sorry," said the woman. "Give it a couple of years, dear. They're showing *Bambi* down the road if you're interested!" I laughed, but in

120

my heart it was raining cats and dogs. How could I have been so stupid as to tell her my real age? The tricky bit was turning round and making a semi-dignified exit through the crowd. I shut my eyes and grabbed Deborah's arm.

"Don't say a word," I hissed, "just follow me out as if nothing has happened." But Deborah had something to say first.

"Since when did I become your sister?" she demanded.

"Not now, Debra!"

"De-BORE-ah, actually!" Then, as I dragged her towards the exit, she made an announcement to the queue that left them in no doubt as to our relationship. "I'm his girlfriend!" she screeched. "And don't let him tell you different. I'm his girlfriend with a capital K. I. S. S!"

My face was glowing like the bottom of a jam pan when I got outside. I couldn't look back directly at my vision in purple, so I pretended to find a tear in my shirt and sneaked a glance at my beloved through my armpit. She had gone, swallowed up by the queue. No doubt dragged away by her jealous date when he saw how much she pined for me.

"Well," I said brusquely to Deborah, "are you going to give me my brooch, now, or what?"

"We haven't had a kiss yet," she answered

flirtatiously, rolling her eyes at me, like two bowls of brown soup in a British Rail Buffet Car. Then she took one step forward and puckered her lips together. I took one step backwards.

"Right," said Deborah. "No kiss, no brooch. So where to now?"

"Can't we just call it a night?" I pleaded.

"No date, no ears," said Deborah, miming a butcher's knife with her hand. Touché, I thought. My sigh was indiscreet, but honest.

"Do you eat?" I asked.

"Everything," she replied.

"Oh dear," I said, fearing as much. I fingered the loose change in my pocket. "There's a greasy spoon round the corner. How do you fancy some chips?"

Well, rather a lot in fact. Deborah took one look at the menu and ordered everything. Prawn cocktail, onion bhaji, oxtail soup, fish pie, sausage, beans, eggs and mash, double bubble and cheeseburger, sweet and sour pork, treacle sponge, jam roly-poly, custard and tea. Her mother had once told her that it was impolite to pick at food on a date, but the truth was she was an out-and-out pig. Deborah's order already covered three pages of the waitress's notepad by the time I was asked what I wanted.

"A glass of water," I smiled weakly. It was all I could afford.

The sight of Deborah gnawing on the bone in her oxtail soup and straining cabbage through her brace reminded me of a natural history film about the eating habits of hippopotami. She made more mess than a muck spreader. The only good thing about her hoglike devotion to the trough was that with her mouth full she couldn't speak to me.

"You want more custard?" The voice of the Greek waitress brought me crashing back to earth. Debra had finished her fourth pudding and was looking distinctly stuffed. She burped, shook her head slowly, and continued chewing. "You want bill?" The waitress was talking to me now. I turned to thank her, but found myself unable to speak. I was zapped by her beauty. If you can imagine having your heart ripped from your chest and ten men playing five-a-side football with it, it felt a bit like that. Her name was Mia. I could read it on the badge pinned to her impressive bosom, in fact I couldn't stop reading it. She had long black hair and dark olive skin and she smelt of bubble 'n' squeak.

MIA

To be so near
To Mia,
I fear
Diarrhoea!

My stomach liquified as I sat prostrate at the altar of her beauty. She had nailed my tongue to the roof of my mouth.

"You want bill?" she repeated. I opened and closed my lips like a dying fish, but no words came out. "Well?" she said.

"Hi," I grunted, waggling my head from side to side like a Thunderbirds puppet. "What's a good-looking doll like you doing in a dump like this?"

"My father owns it," she said.

"Really?" I gulped, wishing I'd kept my big mouth shut. "Nice dump … I mean, place."

"Actually, I think we had better have the bill before I'm sick," groaned Deborah. I charmed Mia with a smile.

"My sister, Debra," I said.

"It's De-BORE-ah, actually," came the expected, but muted response. "And I'm not your sister."

"How much?" I asked, gazing deeply into Mia's sad eyes.

"Thirty-one pounds, twenty-six pence." she said, reading her pad. I didn't flinch.

"How much?" I asked again.

"Thirty-one pounds and twenty-six pence," interjected Deborah. "Have you got a bucket of water I could borrow to rinse through my brace?"

"No," said Mia. "Is there a problem with the bill?"

"A problem?" I said (still smiling). "No. There's no problem. Not with the bill. I mean, the bill's cheap if you consider what my sister's had."

"I'm not his sister!"

"How much you got?" asked Mia.

"Er ... 'bout eleven pounds," I mumbled.

"Then I get the police," she said and she started to go, but Deborah grabbed her arm.

"How about if we paid with this?" she suggested.

"No," I protested. "Anything but that!" But she'd already unpinned Mum's silver brooch and before I could grab it, Mia had it in her hand.

"OK," she said. "It's a deal!" I looked daggers at Deborah, but she sent them straight back with knobs on.

"Sister!" she spat across the table. "I told you you should have kissed me. Shall we go?" I had no choice. It was 10.30 pm and I had to be home by 11.00 before my parents returned from their Harvester's dinner.

I refused to talk to Deborah as I walked her home, which was fine by Deborah because she felt so sick. As we walked up the path to her front door (and monster-Mum removed herself sharpish from the bay window), Deborah span round and clasped me to her chest.

"Forgive me!" she wailed. Her brace had

snagged my hair. Every time she spoke, she wrenched great clumps of it out by the roots. "Do you still love me?"

"No," I said bluntly. What did I care if I hurt her feelings now? She'd given Mum's brooch away when it wasn't hers to give.

"Oh, say that you do, because I still love you." She pulled her head away and took half my scalp with it. Then she smiled alluringly. There was a large piece of gristle stuck between her front teeth. "Make up a love poem for me!"

"No," I said again.

"Oh please," she begged. "Just a teeny tiny sonnet." I saw an opportunity to kill her crush stone dead.

"All right," I said. "If you want a poem, you can have one.

De-BORE-ah's face is just like the moon,
All yellow and big and cheesy.
But the moon rules the tides
And the tides rule the waves,
And the waves, like her face, make me queasy."

Deborah swooned and fainted. Apparently, it was the most beautiful thing she'd ever heard (since Friday's dinner bell, I'll bet). What was wrong with this girl? Even when I insulted her to her face, she still loved me! I knocked on the door and got her psychopathic, blade-packing mother to drag her out of my sight, before making my excuses and hightailing out of there like a turbo-powered cheetah running on high octane curry powder.

I could hardly believe that my diabolical night with Deborah was finally at an end. One thing was for sure; I'd remember this date for the rest of the week.

I got home with minutes to spare. I crept around the back of the house and carefully let myself in through the back door, holding the latch down to avoid any loud clicks. I was expecting the kitchen to be empty, so I got the shock of my life when I turned round to find Nan and Sherene still sitting at the table, staring at three platefuls of freezing cold dinner.

"Oh Hallelujah, the bog boy weturnth!" mocked Sherene, accompanying the heavy irony with a burst of slow hand-clapping.

"Ah, there you are," said Nan. "Where did you get to? I thought you'd fallen down the toilet!"

"You shouldn't have waited," I said, surveying the congealed lumps of something-nasty that Nan had lovingly prepared. I used a fork to tap a grey lump of food that had long since set like a brick. I bent the fork. "It looks lovely," I gagged, "but I'm not hungry."

"Nonthenthe," bullied Sherene. "If I've got to eat it, tho have you!" I shot a hateful stare

127

at my sister and pulled up a kitchen chair.

"I thought you'd have finished hours ago," I said.

"It's rude to start before everyone's seated," said Nan. "Still, you're here now, so we can begin."

"What is it?" I asked casually, turning over a chunk of green fur to see if it had little hairy legs underneath. Nan smiled and rubbed her stomach.

"It's delicious and ever so good for you," she slurped.

"It'th thteamed thtomach," announced Sherene, "with thproutth." I foolishly thought that if I changed the subject Nan might forget about the food on our plates.

"Mum and Dad not home?" I asked, but Nan took her babysitting duties seriously, and would not hear another word until we had finished every last mouthful.

Although I say it myself, my sleight of hand during the next ten minutes was magnificent. I managed to shovel all of my food under the table without Nan or Sherene noticing. By the time Mum and Dad came home, Pongo had gobbled up my steamed sheep's stomach with gusto and was now regretting it. His large intestine was rumbling like a freight train carrying nuclear waste, and was straining to erupt like a corked volcano. Luckily, I recognized the tell-tale gusts of wind that preceded such

128

an explosion, and managed to get the bubbling
bloodhound outside into the garden before he
damaged Mum's kitchen units.

We were sent to bed immediately. Sherene was
allowed to leave what she couldn't eat (which
was everything), which rather cheesed me off
as I'd gone to such trouble to clear my plate.
Mum was still crying and Dad looked rather
fed up, so it was Nan who came upstairs to
kiss us goodnight.

"Nan," I said, as she pecked my forehead
and shuffled towards the light switch, "just
suppose, and this hasn't happened to me, obviously, but supposing you'd given somebody
you loved something that didn't belong to you
and they'd given it to somebody else, whom
you didn't love and never could, because it
would be like kissing a chip basket in a deep
fat fryer, and then they'd given it to a third
person, whom you also loved, but only for a
couple of hours, you know, and this person
thought it was theirs, but it wasn't, and the
person who owned this thing in the first place
was going to explode her brains all over breakfast if she ever found out that you'd given this
thing away in the first place ... could I be
wrong in assuming that you should get this
thing back at any cost?"

"Assuming this person was your mother,"
whispered Nan, plunging the room into dark-

ness, "I'd say yes, Johnny. Get the brooch back. Sweet dreams!" And she shut the door, leaving me wondering how on earth she'd known what I was talking about.

ON THE COMPLEXITY OF NANS

How do they know,
These Nans in the attic?
How can they think
When their brains are erratic?
How is it what they say always
makes sense,
When saying it makes them sound
awfully dense?

(Johnny Casanova — wracked with guilt and night sweats)

I couldn't work out what was keeping me awake most that night, my guilt at losing Mum's brooch or Pongo's howling. His late-night snack under the table appeared to have disagreed with his digestive tract. At four o'clock in the morning his floodgates burst. The explosion was heard fifteen miles away, and within seven minutes an emergency team from the Bomb Squad was scouring our garden for shrapnel. They found nothing, of course, just a weak but relieved bloodhound asleep on the lawn next to my Dad's shed, which had been freshly pebbledashed from roof to floor in masticated tripe.

ON THE IMMINENT FAILURE OF
DAD'S SENSE OF HUMOUR

Troubles
Come in bubbles
When a doggle's
Over-fed.
Especially
When the doggle's
Blown his bubbles
On Dad's shed.

(Johnny Casanova — waiting for the
shouting to start)

12
KISS AND MAKE-UP

The next morning was Saturday and we were all up early. Pongo's midnight blitz had ensured that none of us got any sleep and Dad was keen to swab down his shed before he went shopping at GnomeBase. Mum was wandering around the kitchen in slow motion, suffering from a depressive condition that Dad called The Valium.

"All right, ducks?" she wobbled, trying to smile, but the smile kept slipping off the side of her face. She was trying to make breakfast and do the washing at the same time, and both activities were clearly beyond her. She put the toast in the washing machine and spin-dried it into a thousand soggy pieces. She spread Marmite on Sherene's dungarees, poured washing powder into the sugar shaker and served up bowls of crispy socks instead of cornflakes. I tactfully tried to point out her mistake by

132

thrusting the sock under her nose, but she wasn't in the mood for jokes.

"If you don't like cornflakes, then have Shredded Wheat instead," she barked, tipping the crispy socks into the rubbish bin and plonking two Brillo pads into my bowl instead. As I sat there contemplating the tufts of fine wire poking out through the milk, I realized that if we were ever to be a normal family again, it was up to me to retrieve Mum's brooch before sundown. I was just about to make an excuse to leave the table, so I could go upstairs to flush my Brillo pads down the loo, when Mum suddenly rounded on me. She was holding a bottle of nit lotion in her left hand. Sherene gagged on her mug of warm, milky fabric softener.

"Oh bwilliant!" she squealed with glee. "You're for the smelly hairwash, Johnny! Ha, ha, ha!"

"Shut up!" said Mum. "Johnny, bend forward and put your head on the table."

"But I haven't got nits," I protested, "and I've told you, I don't want that stuff anywhere near my hair. It's sacred!" But Mum was in no mood to argue. She grabbed my arm and pushed my neck down onto the table. I had to act fast. Pongo was lying in the sin bin underneath the breakfast bar, his head hung in shame after last night. He thumped his tail as I looked at him and lazily scratched his stomach with his hind leg. "There!" I yelled. "Look at Pongo. He's got nits. You don't want to waste the last of that stuff on me. Give it to him!" Mum was momentarily distracted by Pongo lurching to his feet. "Here, let me," I said, snatching the bottle out of her hands and sprinkling the remains of the lotion over Pongo's back.

"No, Johnny, don't!" shouted Mum, but it was too late. The lotion went to work on Pongo's skin like a demon dose of itching powder. The dog went frantic. He span around on the spot like a mohair jumper on a rotating washing line and tried to scratch his back with all four paws at the same time (a technical impossibility, of course), which brought him crashing down on his belly, causing him to whistle a wet one before any of us had moved. In the ensuing panic, as Mum tried to kick Pongo out of the back door and Sherene pretended to be sick in the sink, I slipped away from the table and rushed upstairs.

Ten minutes later, I had re-gelled my hair and was hanging my new "BEWARE – I might just have a woman in here!" poster on my bedroom door, when Sherene appeared at the top of the stairs and started to cry.

"What is it now?" I asked.

"Mummy'th going to die!" she bawled, dramatically.

"No, she isn't," I said. "She's just having a bad day, that's all."

"OK then, Mr Cool," she said, challengingly, "anthwer me thith. If you had to thave Mum'th life…"

"I have to know what she's going to die from, first," I said, hoping to annoy Sherene with my interruption, which I did. She jumped on my back and thumped me as hard as she could between the shoulder blades. She wanted a big red bus to drop out of the sky and squash my fat head flat, apparently.

"I hate you, I hate you, I hate you! You gweat, big, thlimy, ugly, windbag of a doo-dah. I only want to athk you a quethtion."

"Well, ask it then," I guffawed. She climbed down off my back and straightened out her dress.

"Right. If you had to thave Mum'th life would you give her back the bwooch that you took?" That was my cue to stop laughing.

"Who says I took it?" I asked, defensively.

"Me, because I thaw you, you gweat big cowpat. You weren't exactly Mr Clever-Thief about it. It'th all becauthe of you that Mum'th gone mad."

"Well, I haven't got it anymore," I said. "I lost it last night."

"Well, you'll jutht have to get it back then, won't you? 'Cauthe if you don't, Mum might have to thpend the wetht of her life locked up

135

in a thmelly old mad-houthe with ratth and beetleth and a bucket to pooh in!" Sherene had a gift for painting unpleasant pictures in the mind and Mum in a loony bin was one of the more successful ones.

"It won't be easy," I said. "You'll have to help me." Sherene nodded in a slow, deliberate way that she thought made her look grown-up, but inside I could see she was turning girly cartwheels. This was the first time that her elder brother-hero (that's me) had ever spoken to her like an adult and she was loving every minute of it. "There's a woman involved," I admitted, "and it's her heart we have to win to get to the brooch. Only she's not like all the rest."

"Why?" asked Sherene. "Hath thhe got thwee headth?"

"She's seventeen!" I said, sucking in my cheeks to stop myself from grinning like a manhole cover. Sherene gasped like I knew she would. I carried on impressing her. "So, we're going to need clothes, Dready clothes, and make-up – lots of it."

"Make-up?" echoed Sherene, with eyes as round as gobstoppers.

"When I walk out of this door, Sherene, I've got to look chicer than a sheik because, believe me, if I make a move on her and she susses out I'm only packing thirteen years, she's going to eat me alive, and I mean todo scrunchymunchy! We're talking street cred here, got it? Cowboy boots, aftershave, the lot!"

"Cor!" Sherene trembled with excitement. "You're the bethtetht brother I've got, Johnny Wormth!"

"Casanova," I corrected her. "Casanova's the name and don't you forget it!"

Sherene and I took one hour to make me look older. The cowboy boots were a stroke of genius. They raised me up by three inches and took me over that magic five-foot marker that separates men from boys. I tucked my jeans into the top of the boots to accentuate my ruggedness and left my "Free the Herb!" T-Shirt hanging loose like a potato sack.

"How about a nice tie?" said Sherene.

"Get real!" I told her. "There's old and there's old!"

"Yeth, but you thtill only look about fifteen," she said. "You need thomething elthe."

"How about one of Dad's cardigans?" I said.

"Ooh yeth! You'll look like Clark Kent on hith day off," she swooned. I nicked a fawn one with fake leather buttons from the airing cupboard. Sherene gave it eleven and a half out of ten and then asked what jewellery I was planning to wear.

"I've got a gold medallion," I said, rummaging through my Aston Martin piggy-bank for my World Cup coin that had cost me seven hundred Tiger Tokens at our local garage. It looked great on my chest from a distance, but up close it didn't cut the mustard. Des Walker's face was clearly visible on one side and on the other there was a Bulldog in football boots.

"Doethn't matter," said Sherene. "Thhe won't be getting clothe enough to thee that." I was miffed by her snide implication.

"Oh, yes she will!" I said. "By the time I've buttered her up, she'll be closer to me than a licked stamp on an envelope." I would have given Sherene a lesson in just exactly how sexy I was to teenage girls, but we still had my make-up to do and I couldn't afford to upset her. The thinking behind the make-up was to accentuate my luxuriant facial hair until it looked like I had a natural moustache and sideburns. Sherene pasted lashings of Mum's mascara on to my top lip with Dad's toothbrush. "Do you think that's too much?" I asked, surveying her broad brush strokes in the mirror.

"No. I wouldn't have done it if I did," she replied.

"You don't think it looks like I've got a dead squirrel curled round my mouth?"

"I think it lookth vewy manly!" stated Sherene. Actually I thought so too, but I just needed reassurance. And the sideburns were certainly good enough to pass the "casual glance in the mirror test". If I swung my head from side to side in front of the mirror and just sort of happened to catch sight of my side-burns, they looked pretty effective and not obviously painted on at all.

I tiptoed across the landing into the bath-room and retrieved the fake brooch from the rubbish bin. I was going to exchange it for the real one and hope Mia wouldn't notice. Then I crept downstairs into the hall, slipped on a pair of Mum's shades to turn me into a hip-hop-homeboy and admired the full effect of my Dready gear in the mirror. I had to admit that the clothes did the trick. Not only did I look old enough to go to university but, if I was Mia, I'd want to eat me. There was still something missing, however.

"A bwiefcathe?" suggested Sherene.

"Too crumbly."

"An umbwella?"

"Too yuppie."

"Then how about a thcarf?"

"Too mumsy," I said, dismissively. "I want something to make me look like a real man!"

"Another body?" said Sherene.

"I've got it!" I said. "A rottweiler! Some-thing powerful and snarling on the end of my fist, something untamed and primitive that screams to the world: Hey! If you think my dog's macho, you should try me!"

And that was how Pongo came to be scratching his back on the pavement outside the greasy spoon cafe, twenty-five minutes later. A sign on the door above his head read, NO DOGS ALLOWED, which had rather put my rottweiler out in the cold, while I made my move on Mia.

ON LOOKING GOOD FOR GIRLS

To keep the girls happy
Don't strap on a nappy
And don't wear a pink baby-gro.
Jeans are appealing,
But not when you're kneeling,
Lest you want your bottom to show.
A shell suit's two leerious,
A pin stripe too serious,
Bow ties make you look like a fool.
There's only one way
To make a girl's day,
Wear a fridge and she'll think you
look cool.

(Johnny Casanova — looking hard to-the-max and at least 172)

13
MIA'S TEARS

The cafe was empty. I sat at a table near the door and looked butch. Mr Patel's plastic brooch was in my pocket, ready to be swapped back, but Mia was nowhere to be seen. I could wait. I hitched my cowboy boots up on to the table and sucked on a toothpick to pass the time, sliding it into the corner of my mouth and rolling it across my tongue like a Clint Eastwood cigar. Still the little lady didn't show, so I nibbled at the edges and squeezed the moist wood between my molars, pulping it flat until it frayed at the end into a thousand tiny splinters, which broke away from the main shaft and floated on a tide of saliva into all those difficult-to-get-at places in my mouth. It was harder than it looked, this tooth-pick-chewing. I was using a second toothpick to winkle out the first, when Mia appeared over my shoulder and took out her notepad.

She gave me such a fright that I swallowed both picks at the same time and coughed myself half to death for five whole minutes.

"What you want?" asked Mia, as my shades demisted. I smiled beguilingly at her, but she flicked her swollen red eyes away. Was that a tear I saw? So, she was playing the vulnerable card. The little minx. I gave her my best pick-up line.

"I'll have a strong black coffee," I drawled. "'cause that's how I like my women!"

"Anything else?" she asked, apparently unaware of my presence.

"A sticky doughnut," I grunted, half closing my eyes to look mean and moody, "'cause that's how I like my doughnuts!" I had expected some response to my witty retort, but she left the table without saying a word. While she was busy behind the counter, I took a paper napkin out of the stainless steel rack on the table, and wrote a love poem on the back. When Mia returned with my coffee and doughnut, I slipped it into her hand and told her that true love could not be denied.

MIA AMORE

Mia, Mia,
My heart is on fire.
Is yours for hire?
Or can I buy it?

She finished reading the napkin, slapped me hard about the cheeks and rushed into the kitchen, leaking tears like a machine-gunned water butt.

Five minutes later, I was still sitting there, stunned by the blow, when a large Greek man, with a grey moustache that twitched on his top lip like a prize-fighting mouse, stormed up to my table. He grabbed Dad's cardigan in both hands, lifted my feet off the ground and dangled me in mid-air. His bulbous nose was inches away from mine as he fired Greek insults through my skull. I guessed he was Mr Theopopilopolus, Mia's father, by the number of times he mentioned Mia's name, and I guessed too that I had done something to offend her, by the way he grasped me by the seat of my jeans and deposited me outside his cafe like a bag of rancid rubbish.

Now you can call me paranoid if you like, you can call me permanently pessimistic or even Master Boring Old Fart Who Always Looks On The Dark Side Of Life, but I got the distinct impression that Mia didn't like me. It was hard to put my finger on exactly where I'd gone wrong, but somewhere along the line I'd confused love at first sight with blind hatred and from then on a meaningful relationship had never really been an option. Sadly, the upshot of my failure to seduce Mia meant that I now had to return home without Mum's diamond brooch, which for lots of reasons (not the least of which being that Mum would be locked up in a padded cell) was not going to be popular.

"Come on, Pongo," I sighed, dragging the shaky hound to his feet by the scruff of his itchy neck, "let's go home and face the music."

We made a sorry pair, Pongo and I, as we shuffled off down the street and turned into the alleyway that double-backed along the rear of the cafe. All my efforts to retrieve Mum's brooch had come to nothing and I hadn't even got a snog to show for it. Perhaps I was gay. Maybe all the girls knew something I didn't. I mean, something had to be wrong with me, when the only girl who half-way fancied me was a metal detector's dream with a face like St Pancras Station. Pongo squeaked a sympathetic parp in my direction as he wagged his tail. Nobody loved him either.

"I do," I said, rubbing the top of his head and covering my hand in nit lotion. I couldn't hate Pongo now. I was for the firing squad when I got home and he was the only friend I'd got.

As we sloped past a pair of large industrial dustbins, I heard a noise behind a tall pile of cardboard packing cases. It was a gentle sobbing. I edged closer and spotted a pair of legs; long, brown, shiny legs like Sherene's Barbie doll. I recognized them immediately. They

were Mia's. She was sitting on a cooking fat
tin weeping into a paper napkin and on the
napkin was my poem. She looked up as I shuffled into view towing my decrepit dog behind
me. I sheepishly removed my shades and
stared at the ground, half expecting her to hit
me again.

"Sorry," I said, breaking the long silence. "I
didn't mean to upset you." And suddenly Mia
was in my arms. I dropped Pongo's lead in
terror. She had her head on my shoulder and
was shuddering uncontrollably, soaking my
Dready T-shirt with her tears. My poem had
obviously hit the spot, but what was I supposed to do now? Where was I supposed to
put my hands? I couldn't leave them hanging
rigidly by my side, like two metal rods. She'd
think I didn't like her if I didn't comfort her
with a hug and a cuddle. And what if she tried
to kiss me? What if I bit her tongue by mistake? I glared at Pongo, who had rolled over
on to his back and was showing off his floppy
back bits. I wanted him to tuck them away in
case they put Mia off and made her stop, but
Pongo was not renowned for his modesty and
the more I glared, the more he whined with
pleasure at seeing me in the clutches of a red
hot chickeroo. I could feel her warm breath on
my chest. It was making my feet sweat. She
lifted her head off my shoulder and my nervous system went into spasm. This was it.

My first frenchie! My ears were pounding like jungle drums as my blood pressure burst through the top of my skull. I gulped for air as her forehead passed in front of my eyes and her hands moved slowly up my back. Oh, my God, what if I had bad breath? I hadn't brushed my teeth before I came out. Who cared? Her silken hair had just flicked the tip of my nose and made it tingle. No wonder the Eskimos were nuts about noses...

"Oh, Mia!" I shouted, tossing back my head and pursing my lips, "Mama Mia!"

But she wasn't there. She was standing ten feet away, blowing her nose on my poem.

"I so sorry," she sobbed, "but I so sad. I just needed someone to hold me."

Perhaps she hadn't been trying to kiss me, after all.

"You've got mascara all down your cheek," I said tenderly, a few seconds later, when Mia had calmed down.

"But I don't wear make-up," she replied in a trembling voice. I ran the sleeve of Dad's cardigan across my top lip and streaked the cuff black.

"Oh," I cringed, "it was mine." She gave me a strange look, like I was a pervert or something. "I don't normally wear it, you understand... It's just that, you know ... well, you know." It's not easy explaining to a girl you fancy why you're wearing your Mum's make-up. "I'm thinking of joining the army, so I was just practising for night manoeuvres with the old face-camouflage stuff, you see. Anyway, you're probably wondering why I'm here?"

"No," she sighed.

"Oh." I was going to tell her anyway. "It's about that brooch I lent you last night. Remember?"

"The one your girlfriend gave me?"

"She is NOT my girlfriend!" I exclaimed. "Anyway, she didn't exactly give it to you, you see. It was meant to be more of a short-term loan. I was wondering if I could possibly have it back?"

"No." She didn't mince her words.

"No. OK. Fine… It's just that, well, you see, it belongs to my mother, and she insisted that I… Er… " I hoped she'd see reason, but she didn't.

"No," she said, shaking her head. "It belongs to my great-grandmother now."

"Well, I'm sure she'd understand," I pleaded.

"I doubt it," replied Mia. "My great-granny is dead. I give her the brooch as something special for her to wear on her last journey. She was a beautiful old woman and now she is at the Purley Gates."

"Well, better Heaven than Hell," I quipped, nervously.

"No, the Purley Gates in Purley. Is a chapel of rest. Tomorrow we bury her… Oh, great-granny! I do so miss her!" She burst into tears again, while I hovered uneasily in front of her and tried to think of something comforting to say, which was pretty hard as I'd never met the dead woman.

"That's a bit of a bummer," I said, cheerily, trying to raise Mia's spirits. And then to fill the awful silence that followed, "Have you met my dog, Pongo?" Pongo scratched his neck and gusted a breeze from his nether regions, at which point Mia fled indoors, dropping my poem on the ground as she went.

"Well, thanks a bunch, Pongo," I snapped, after the back door to the cafe had slammed shut. "You've put her off me now!" Pongo wagged his tail and arched his neck against the ground, which was his subtle way of telling me that it was fine by him if I wanted to spend the next three and a half hours rubbing his tummy. I had no such plans. "Ever been to Purley?" I asked. Pongo barked twice. "Well, you have now. Come on, we've got a brooch to swap!" Unfortunately, Pongo could not get up. His back legs were knackered. "Look, I can't just leave you here," I complained. Pongo smiled. It sounded like a splendid plan to him. "I might need your tracking skills to find the chapel of rest." He sniffed the ground and shook his head, sadly. "Yes, all right, so you can't smell anything anymore, but you're coming with me, whether you like it or not!"

Ten minutes later, I staggered out of the alleyway dragging Pongo behind me. I had strapped the old bloodhound to a scuffed-up skateboard that I'd found in one of the dustbins and, while I struggled to tow his weight, he sighed contentedly and closed his eyes to make the journey to Purley pass more quickly.

ON SKATEBOARDS AND DOGS
IN PUBLIC

A man with cow pats on his head
Rather wishes he was dead.
I know exactly how he feels,
When I pull Pongo round on wheels.

(Johnny Casanova — dying of
embarrassment on Purley High
Street)

14
STANDING AT THE PURLEY GATES

The Purley Gates Chapel of Rest (just off
Purley Way, between Alf Tupper – The Butcher
and Marjorie Marjoram's Decorative Flower
Shop) was extremely well signposted. "This
way to Heaven" said a large pink sign wired
to the lamppost in front of the chapel and
another, facing the other way down the street,
read: "Knocking on the Pearly Gates? Quick!
Come inside and check our rates."

It was only once I'd arrived that I realized I
needed a plan of action. Somehow I'd have to
get the undertaker to let me see Mia's great-
granny alone, so I could swap the brooches.
It was a toss-up between claiming to be her
great-grandson with a highly infectious dose
of mumps, or a kind-hearted neighbour bringing great-granny's emotionally challenged dog
to pay his last tearful respects in private. Both

150

sounded plausible to me. I was standing outside the flower shop using the window as a
mirror to wipe off Mum's mascara when a
hand tapped me on the shoulder. It was
Ginger, or at least he would have been ginger
if he'd had any hair. His head was completely
bald, like a freshly boiled egg.

"Shut it," he glowered. "I'm not in the
mood!"

"I didn't say a word," I said, trying not to
laugh.

"This is your sister's doing, this is!" he
sulked, slapping his shiny scalp. "Gave me her
nits, didn't she!"

"You can get a lotion for that," I said, helpfully. "Cures all known nits, even on dogs!"
Pongo was not amused and bit my ankle.

"You could get a lotion, once," corrected
Ginger. "Only there's been such a run on the
stuff at the chemists' that they haven't got any
left, so my mum had me shaved instead!"

"Have you ever thought of being a rugby
ball when you grow up?" I sniggered.

"Go on, laugh yourself sick," he said, "but
just you wait till it happens to you."

"It won't," I said. "Never. Pigs'll fly before
I let anyone come near my hair with a razor.
These locks are sacred, mate. They're like
Samson's. If they're cut off, I lose all my
pulling power."

"Oh, yes. How was the date with Alison?"

151

he asked suddenly.

"Went like a dream," I lied. Then I swiftly changed the subject. "Have you got ten minutes?"

"Not for you, no."

"Good, 'cause I need your help."

"To do what?"

"To find a dead body," I said.

"What!" Ginger's eyebrows jumped off the front of his face. "You must be joking!"

"No. There's an old woman in there who's wearing Mum's brooch. Me and Pongo were just about to go in and get it, weren't we, boy?" My fearless sidekick had drifted off to sleep.

"Dead bodies smell, don't they?" scowled Ginger.

"No worse than Pongo," I replied. "Anyway, they do things to dead people nowadays to stop them from smelling."

"Like what?"

"Well, like ... I don't know... Wash them, I suppose. Squirt Lemon Jif behind their ears. Fill them up with pot pourri. Your guess is as good as mine." I could see Ginger was still reluctant. "Look, if you help, I promise not to call you a slaphead at school." That made his mind up. He was on!

Inside the Purley Gates it was dead quiet. The first person I saw was the receptionist, sitting directly opposite where we'd come in. She was really neat. All her clothes were tucked in tight, like she was trying to make herself smaller. Her hair was wound up in a tiny bun on the top of her head, and her specs had bottle-thick lenses that made her eyes look huge, like two fried eggs. But she was still a woman and, as such, potentially susceptible to the allure of my Dready gear, which was just as well, because somehow I had to get past her to reach Great-granny Theopopilopolus.

As I walked towards the reception desk, a middle-aged woman came out of one of the six identical doors that led to the chapels of rest. Her head was bowed. Her nose was buried in a sopping wet handkerchief.

"Cheer up," I said. "It may never happen."
But it obviously had.

"What do you want?" hissed the receptionist, who looked like she'd never seen a pair of cowboy boots, a bald boy, or a dog on a skateboard before. "Dead pets should be taken to the vet," she said. Pongo had leaked in his sleep and was surrounded by a fruity canine scent from the bowels of Beelzebub himself!

"He's not dead," I explained. "Bit of a seepage problem with his lower gut." Then I leant across her desk and offered her my hand. "Hi. Johnny Casanova's the name. Do you mind?..." I reached forward and slid her glasses off the end of her nose. "What's a beautiful girl like you doing in a place like this?" I smouldered, while she scrabbled desperately for her specs.

"Stop that," she squinted. "I can't see a thing! Where are they?"

"Sorry," I said, handing them back, "just looking. Tell me, is Mrs Theopopilopolus in?"

"I'd be surprised if she wasn't," replied the receptionist, sarcastically. "She can hardly get up and walk out of here, can she? Why do you want to know?"

"I need to see her," I explained.

"Yes, well, if you wait a moment, I'll get the manager. He makes all the difficult decisions around here," she said prissily, clip-clopping out from behind her desk and through a door marked "Private".

This was our chance. I unstrapped Pongo from the skateboard and gave Ginger the low-down. "Right, come on!" I said. "We've got one minute to find her before the manager chucks us out."

Ginger tried the first door, but it was locked. The second door opened, but the stiff was a six-foot man with tattoos and a beard. The third room was empty. The fourth room was full of dancing girls and vicars.

"Very kinky," sniggered Ginger. I had to drag him away. By the time we'd reached the fifth door, Pongo was pooped. His tongue flopped out of his mouth like the tail fin of a stunned red mullet. Behind the door we found a troop of circus performers staring at a coffin that was swinging from the ceiling by two wires.

"Dead trapeze artist," I said. "Last room. Come on." And there she was, Great-granny Theopopilopolus, stretched out in her coffin as if she was asleep and pinned to the lapel of her suit jacket was the object of my quest, Mum's antique diamond brooch. "Yes!" I whispered excitedly. "Way to go!" As Ginger and I leant over the grey corpse, Pongo staggered through the doorway, weaving drunkenly from side to side, looking for a comfy spot to rest his aching limbs. While we wrestled with the brooch pin, he propped his forelegs on the side of the coffin and looked inside. Then, just as Ginger released the pin from its catch, Pongo scrabbled up the side of the coffin, flopped over the edge and fell on top of Great-granny Theopopilopolus's chest, trapping Ginger's hands. At that moment the manager stormed into the room with a face as puce as beetroot juice.

"What is going on?" he bellowed.

"I think they're grave robbers," piped up the receptionist, who had shadowed him into the chapel. The manager's roar could be heard in Heaven. With one broad sweep, he shoved his huge, hairy hand under Pongo's belly and scooped him off the corpse, but the pressure on the old dog's gut was too much to bear. A megaton tornado blew a storm out of Pongo's rumble seat and blasted the receptionist's top knot clean off the top of her head.

"You don't understand..." Ginger bleated, as the manager hurled Pongo out of the chapel and came back for him. "Tell him why we're here, Johnny!" But I kept my mouth shut and pretended to grieve over the old lady's coffin, because I still had to get Mum's brooch back. Meanwhile poor old Ginger skidded out the front door on his bald head like an ice hockey puck, wishing he'd never got involved in my stupid plan. "I'll get you for this!" he called. "You've stitched me up for the last time, Johnny!" Then the manager came back for me, but he found me kneeling over the body in a pious position of prayer. Being a professional who understood the pain of grief, he had to leave me alone, which I thought was pretty clever thinking on my part. So he calmed down and I muttered something like,

"...and God Bless my dog, Pongo, as well. Amen." And then we talked.

"Who are you?" asked the manager.

"A son," I quivered.

"She doesn't have any sons," he said.

"No, not her son. Just a son ... of someone else altogether... Erm ... I'm the son of..." I broke down into floods of tears to buy myself

156

more time to make up another identity. "I'm
her paperboy!" I choked. "Her beloved paperboy!"

"And the dog?"

"The paperdog," I wept. "Me and the bald
boy used to take it in turns to see that the news
always got through." I faked a bit more blub-
bing. "You don't know how much I'm going
to miss delivering her papers – *The Crawley
Echo, The Kebab Chronicle* and *Squid Weekly*.
She was a great octopus fan, she was. Used to
cut the pictures out of the magazine and pin
them on her wall... Would you mind awfully if
I just had two minutes alone with her?"

"Two minutes," granted the manager,
warily, "and not a second more. Miss Plunkett
will wait with you." Then he retired backwards through the door and left me alone with
the bespectacled shrew, who was struggling to
pin up her hair again.

If I was going to swap the brooches, I'd have
to work fast. I ran my hand seductively
through my hair like the Fonz, pouted my lips
and sauntered over to the Plain-Jane by the
door.

"No, don't!" I said, catching her hand and
causing her hair to tumble round her ears once
more. "Better," I smouldered, flaring my nostrils, sucking in my cheeks and wiggling my
eyebrows to let her know of the passion inside

157

my breast. "You know, Miss Plunkett," I simmered, like a rocket straining to lift off its launch pad, "you've got one hell of a pair of peepers. Are you a model in your spare time, by any chance?"

"What are peepers?" she asked.

"Eyes, Miss Plunkett, great, big, beautiful eyes!" And I removed her glasses for the second time that morning, thereby rendering her almost completely blind. Then, while she stumbled around looking for her specs, I took the plastic brooch out of my pocket and rushed over to the dead Greek granny. But just as I was about to swap the plastic brooch for the real one, the corpse let out an almighty groan and sat up in her coffin. Miss Plunkett screamed while I jumped out of my socks. Waking your mum and dad in bed with a cup of tea was one thing, but waking the dead was serious trouble!

"What's happening now!" bawled the manager as he stormed back into the room.

"She's alive!" gasped Miss Plunkett. "She's alive! She sat up and moaned, like a ghost!"

The manager did not seem at all concerned. "It happens all the time," he said. "Look," and he prodded Great-granny Theopopilopolus in the ribs, whereupon she groaned again. "It's wind and rigor mortis," he said, giving the body a push, "that's all." Mia's great-granny rocked on her bottom, then fell on to her back in the coffin, with her legs sticking straight up in the air. "Now really, the poor lady has suffered quite enough already. I think we should all leave." Well, so did I, but I still hadn't got Mum's brooch back.

"Not with her legs like that, surely," I blurted out, as the manager turned to the door. "I mean, you'll never get the lid on, will you? Shouldn't we straighten her out, first?"

"Oh, very well," said the manager, who was tired of arguing.

"I'll hold down the top half, if you take the legs," I suggested, which meant that while he was busy forcing Great-granny Theopopilopolus's legs back into the lying down position, I had all the time in the world to remove Mum's brooch from the old lady's jacket and replace it with the almost undetectable fake copy from Mr Patel's clucking hen.

As I left the Purley Gates Chapel of Rest, I offered profuse thanks to the manager for his time and patience.

"You have," I said, sneaking a wink at Miss Plunkett, "been a great, big rock of support amidst a stormy sea of sadness." The manager replied that he hoped never to see me, my bald friend or my malodorous dog again, not even when we were dead. And I shook his hand and said that I couldn't have agreed more.

Ginger was waiting for me when I got outside. He was not a happy bunny.

"You're dead!" he said. I pinched my arm to make sure, but I definitely wasn't. "What have you got against me?" He had a bump the size of a golf ball on his forehead.

"Nothing," I said.

"I thought you were my friend."

"I am," I said. "Want a game of football?" I owed Ginger that after all he'd been through for me, but he was having none of it.

"I'd rather play football with a bunch of girls," he said scathingly. This was supposed to be an insult, but I found the notion of ninety minutes of close bodily contact with a bunch of girls rather appealing. I shared this thought with Ginger, but he was not amused. "I'm going to pay you back," he promised. "For the bump, for the bald head, for losing at football, for the lot! You see if I don't!" Then he turned on his heel and stormed off towards the bus stop.

"Oh, by the way, have you seen Pongo?" I shouted after him. Ginger raised two fingers at me over his shoulder, which I took to mean either "yes, twice" or "no".

A hearse was reversing out of the Purley Gates' back yard as I scoured the street for Pongo. The quicker I found him, the quicker I'd be home, and the quicker I was home, the sooner Mum could have her brooch back.

"Pongo!" I shouted. The coffin in the back
of the hearse lurched to the left. "Pongo!" The
lid of the coffin in the back of the hearse
started to open. "PONGO!" And the bloodhound underneath the lid of the coffin in the
back of the hearse wagged his tail so hard that
he let rip with a peachy fruity tooty of mega-
death proportions, which gassed the driver
and sent the hearse spinning towards an early
appointment with the wrecker's yard. There
was barely time to drag Pongo out through the
smashed rear window before the manager of
the Purley Gates came tearing out the front
door.

"Vandals!" he screamed. "Look what you've
done to my hearse!" Pongo and I didn't hang
around to hear anymore. We were out of
there. Off down the street like a couple of hob-
bled mules. Pongo with his creaking back legs
and me toppling off the three-inch heels on my
cowboy boots.

How we made it home without being caught
I'll never know, but as I staggered in through
the back door, clutching Mum's brooch in my
sweaty palm, I felt like the weight of the world
had been lifted off my shoulders. The groaning dead granny, the crashed hearse, Ginger's
naked nut, the slapped face, the metal kiss and
my broken heart all paled into insignificance
when I thought of the joy Mum would feel on

seeing her precious brooch again. I had been blinded by love when I stole it, now it was time to put things right.

MY MUM

My luv for Purple, Mia and Alison
Is like a TV Charity Telethon.
It stretches on for years and years
And always seems to end in tears.
But in the end there is no other
luv to whack the luv of Mother.

(Johnny Casanova - maturer now and far better for it)

15
THE BROOCH FAIRY

When I told Sherene that I'd successfully rescued the brooch, she jumped around my bedroom like a kangaroo in a sack race.

"Goody goody gum-dwopth!" she yelped, leaping off the bed and flinging her arms around my neck.

"Mind my hair," I told her.

"We can have Mummy back now!" she shrieked.

"Mummy never went away."

"Yeth, thhe did. In her head thhe did, tho there, Johnny-No-Brain!" I pushed past Sherene and went into Mum's bedroom, where I sneaked the diamond brooch under her pillow, so that she'd find it when she went to bed that night.

The next morning, I crept downstairs early to be there when Mum came into the kitchen, but to my surprise the table was already laid.

There was fresh coffee brewing on the stove, toast in the toast rack and linen napkins folded neatly by each place setting. We never used napkins. The sun was pouring in through the open back door and there was someone whistling in the garden. I went to see who it was, just as Mum came in carrying a bunch of newly picked daffodils.

"Morning, pumpkin!" she smiled. "What a beautiful day it is!" Then she bent down and kissed me on the top of my head and I saw the diamond brooch pinned to her jumper.

"Good sleep?" I enquired, making small talk until she chose to mention her brooch.

"The best," she chuckled. "I got a visit last night…"

"From a man?" I said, trying to make it sound like I didn't know what she was talking about. Mum broke into peals of laughter.

"Oh, Johnny, no. Don't be so suggestive. No… From a good fairy." I forced a smile. She didn't really believe that, did she? "And look what the lovely little sprite left me." She thrust the brooch into my face and I feigned a tiny bit of shock followed by a huge amount of over-excitement.

"Rough to-the-max!" I whooped, punching the air with my fists.

"It *is* rough to-the-max, isn't it, Johnny? It's monumental as well. Oh, I could die from happiness. I've informed your dad and I've phoned Uncle Stan and told them both to come and celebrate over breakfast!" My plan had worked. Mum didn't suspect a thing and the family was back to normal.

At breakfast, Uncle Stan sat at one end of the table saying things like, "she's a diamond, your Mum", and "go on darlin', give us a kiss!" while Dad sat at the other end touching up his favourite gnome, Norman Hunter, with a tiny pot of enamel paint. Sherene and I sat opposite each other, eating toast till it was coming out of our ears and Pongo lay in front of the washing machine chewing on a chilli salami that Mum had found for him in the fridge. Then Uncle Stan pulled Mum on to his knee and pretended to steal the brooch again by grabbing her jumper while she wasn't look-ing, and Dad pretended that he didn't mind, and Sherene started to say, "Fairyth don't exitht. Tho who do you think put the bwooch back, Johnny?", but I kicked her under the table, so she stopped.

All in all, I can't remember a happier break-fast, with no arguments and a general feeling that Mum was the luckiest woman in the world to own such a beautiful piece of jewel-lery, and Uncle Stan the most generous man in Britain to give it to her.

But you know what they say: nothing comes for free. Enjoy life now, because sooner or later you'll have to pay for it. And sure enough, the bill came ten minutes later. It came in size twelve boots to be precise, and left muddy footprints all over Mum's clean kitchen floor. And when I say the bill I mean the Bill.

Sergeant Sweety was the first policeman through the back door. In my opinion he's misnamed, because he wasn't a sweety at all. He was a huge bear of a man with short hair and a wide, flat forehead that looked like he'd run into a wall. He ignored the polite request on the doormat to Wipe His Feet and charged into the kitchen like a bull in a bee swarm.

"Hold it right there!" he bellowed gruffly, as his crack squad of spotty recruits lined up behind him. "Nobody move!"

"Can't I finithh my toatht?" asked Sherene, "becauthe it'th peanut butter and Marmite, which, ath it happenth, ith my favouwite. Would you like thome?"

"No," bawled Sergeant Sweety, taking one step forward and accidentally treading on Pongo. There was an ominous squelch.

"What is the meaning of this?" demanded my dad, slamming Norman Hunter down on the table and pulling himself up to Sergeant Sweety's navel.

"Never you mind," said the Sergeant, pressing my dad back into his seat with the sheer volume of his voice. "It's him we want!"

"Uncle Stan!" shrieked Mum, draping herself across Uncle Stan's lap in order to protect him. "No. You can't have him. He's mine ... er, ours ... aren't you, pumpkin?"

"What's he done?" I asked.

"Thief," said Sergeant Sweet. "Big jewel robbery in Bond Street. The game's up, Stan. It's chokey for you, my son." The room fell silent as everyone stared at Uncle Stan and tried to work out if he looked like a crook or not. The only sound came from Pongo as his stomach juices churned and he whimpered from the effort of holding it all in. Suddenly, Uncle Stan sprang from his chair like he'd been bitten on the bum by a spider, and tossed Mum onto the floor.

"You'll never take me alive, copper!" he shouted, vaulting Nan, who was on her hands and knees in the hallway, picking up chocolate raisins.

"Quick, after him," ordered Sergeant Sweety as Stan wrenched open the front door and made good his escape. The spotty recruits gave chase, but Mum flung herself in their path, and flattened them like a thin blue line of dominoes.

"No, you can't have him!" she wailed. "Stan Worms is innocent!"

"Stop it, Babs," hissed Dad, "you're showing us up in front of the Constabulary."

"He's your brother!" screamed Mum, as she

struggled to cling on to a young rookie's trousers. "You should be doing this, not me."

"I'm having breakfast," said Dad. "Besides, if Stan is a robber, he can jolly well fight his own battles." By now the spotty recruits had successfully extricated themselves from Mum's clutches and were running down the drive after Uncle Stan, leaving Sergeant Sweety on his own to face the family.

"I'll take that!" he said, bending down and tugging Mum's diamond brooch off her jumper.

"Stop! Thief!" screamed Mum. "Someone call the police, I'm being robbed!"

"I am the police," said Sergeant Sweety, "and this brooch is evidence. Good day to you." And off he strode, all smug and victorious, to catch up with his spotty troops. He'd only got as far as the front door, however, when Nan popped up in front of him and thrust the faded velveteen birthday card into his hands.

"Don't go, Sweety," she begged. "It's a fair cop. You've got me bang to rights. Lock me up and throw away the key!"

"And good morning to you too, madam," said the slightly confused copper. "Now if you'll excuse me…"

"I'll come quietly," said Nan, but Sweety didn't want her to come anywhere, especially not with him.

"I'm sure that won't be necessary," he said,

patting Nan on the head. She winked and gave him her most charming toothless smile.

"You couldn't give us a kiss first, though, could you?" And she launched herself forward to pucker Sweety on the lips, but he was too quick for her. He ducked underneath her grasp, slipped through the front door, and sprinted down the garden path. Once he'd reached the safety of the street, he turned and delivered his parting shot.

"You're mad," he said. "The whole family. You're completely round the twist!" And then he was off, before Nan could make up the ground between them and force him to eat a fistful of half-chewed chocolate raisins.

I'd never seen a dog sweat before, but Pongo was doing it. Just above his eyebrows, little beads of the stuff, dripping down his cheeks as he strained to put a cork in the mother of all windypops. It was an odd thing to notice, but I was looking at Pongo, because I didn't dare look at Mum. Ten minutes earlier she'd been the happiest woman alive, but now she'd lost everything. It was hardly surprising she'd flipped.

When she got up off the floor, her platinum hair was sticking out like a wire brush and her mad, staring eyes were as big as meat plates. It's not a pretty sight when a beautiful woman lets herself go, and Mum had definitely gone.

169

She picked up the toast rack and hurled it at my dad, which brought his head up sharply from his paint pots.

"There, there," he said. "These things happen, Babs. I'm sorry that your brooch was stolen, but I can't say I'm surprised. Stan always was a bit of a tearaway." She lit a cigarette and blew the smoke in Dad's face. "Now there's no need for that, dear." Sherene and I exchanged a glance. It was that word 'dear'. It didn't mean dear at all, it meant "stupid woman" or "I wish I'd never married you" or "go and kiss a croccodile, why don't you?" Whenever Dad called Mum "dear" it always ended in tears. And today was no exception.

"Dear!" screamed Mum. "'DEAR!' Don't you 'dear' me, you pathetic little man. Call yourself a husband? A real husband wouldn't give his wife nicotine flavoured chewing gum for her birthday, a real husband would buy his wife a diamond brooch!"

"I'll get you another one then," Dad said, defensively.

"I don't want a diamond brooch from you! You think more of those stupid gnomes than you think of me and that's the truth."

"Now, don't bring Norman into this," quivered Dad. "He's very sensitive is Norman. He'll crack up if you call him names!"

"I wish he would crack up! I wish he'd crack

up and disintegrate into dust, that's what I wish!"

"Anyone for more tea?" I chipped in. I was trying to calm the pair of them down, but I don't think I quite timed it right.

"And you can shut up and all!" barked Mum. "Sitting there with your head full of nits! Too vain to let me put the killing lotion in your hair! You're as pathetic as your father, Johnny."

"But my hair's sacred," I said.

"Cows are sacred, Johnny, not hair!" Now she was just being daft. How could a cow be sacred if you couldn't comb it in the morning?

"Just leave the boy alone," snapped Dad. "You're upset, Babs, that's all. It's understandable, but you must calm down." Suddenly, the kitchen shook like Concorde had landed in the front room. There was a deep rumble followed by a massive sonic boom and it was only when Pongo let out a howl that would have scared the socks off the Hound of the Baskervilles that we realized what had happened. The chilli salami had done its worst and poor old Pongo had just delivered a back-end faster-blaster that measured ten on the Richter scale. It peeled the lino off the floor and brought the conversation to a grinding halt. Not for long though, because as the fug cleared the damage was there for all to see. Norman Hunter lay in pieces on the table. His

171

newly painted head had been blown clean off and was bobbing around in Dad's cup of tea. Now it was his turn to flip his lid.

"Norman!" he wailed. "No! Don't leave me, Norman! I love you!" Pongo knew the score and let himself out of the back door, before he was thrown out, but Dad followed him into the garden, brandishing the bread knife. "I'll get you for this, Pongo," he ranted. "I'll put cyanide in your Winalot! Get out of this house and never come back. I disown you, do you hear me? From this day forward, you're no dog of mine!"

"Oh, calm down!" said Mum, disappearing into the garden after Dad. "These things happen, Terry. We can buy you another one." Mum and Dad were like a couple of records stuck in a groove. Round and round, trotting out the same old arguments time after time, and tomorrow it'd be the usual kiss and make up routine as well. I shrugged and shook my head.

"Grown-ups, eh?" I said.

"Gwown-upth, eh?" replied Sherene.

"Who'd have 'em?"

"Who'd have 'em?" she mused.

"So what do we do now?" I asked.

"Tho what do we do now?" was her reply.

"Are you copying everything I say?" I said.

"Are you copying evewything I thay?" said Sherene.

"You flipping are," I shouted.

"I'm flipping not," said Sherene. "I'm ag-weeing with you. Can I athk you a quethtion?"

"No," I said.

"No, lithen, it'th important."

"A million pounds says it isn't."

"A trillion poundth thayth it ith! Lithten, Johnny, pleathe!"

"All right!" I fumed. "What is it?"

"If you were thtuck on a dethert island and only had one pair of girlth knickerth with you..." I'd heard enough and stood up. "No, lithen. If you were on a dethert island and only had one pair of girlth knickerth with you, would you make them into a flag to wave for help or put them on?" Sherene looked at me seriously and waited for my answer. I couldn't believe I was giving her the time of day.

"I'd put them on," I said, just to keep her happy, and I left the room with Sherene's howls of laughter ringing in my ears.

I went round the front of the house to get my bike. Dad was in the garden, building a zip-less isolation tent for Pongo out of bamboo poles and half a mile of cling film, while Mum was arguing over the fence with Mrs Roberts, our next door neighbour, who was waving a dead gerbil in Mum's face. It was her daughter's, apparently, and had been exercising in the garden when Pongo dropped the Big F. The ensuing gas cloud had asphyxiated the pet rodent like a canary in a coal mine, and now

173

Mrs Roberts wanted compensation. I hopped on my bike and cycled off round the block. I needed space to think. If love meant boring old fights all the time, maybe I'd do better to pack women in now, before I got in too deep. Maybe I should phone up Alison and Mia and my vision in purple and tell them to forget all about me. Maybe I should become a monk. Or maybe I should just go and live on my own on a desert island and wear girls knickers all the time!

PHILOSOPHICAL POEM
NUMBER ONE

If luv is like a bed of roses
What smells so sweet and pure,
Why's it so,
To make them grow,
Roses need manure?

(Johnny worms — delving deep where others merely scratch the surface)

16
RED HOT SEX POT

I decided to give up the name Casanova. I hadn't exactly noticed girls beating a path to my door since I started using it. Besides, Worms was a good old traditional English name, earthy and dependable, and some girls liked that too. I was pondering this and other ways to master the fickle love-trap, when I found myself cycling past Mr Patel's SHOP HERE PLEASE shop. He had installed a new digital advertising sign in the window, which promised SLASHED PRICES! UNBELIEVABLE BARGAINS! and RELIGIOUS STATUES ON SALE NOW! BUY TWO AND GET ONE FREE! Mr Patel rushed out to greet me as I stopped to admire his magnificent new toy.

"Mr Johnny, sir," he shouted, waving his arms in the air. "Please to stop! I am having some most memorable news for you."

175

"What?" I said.

"It is all done!" he grinned. I looked at him blankly.

"Good," I said. "What is?"

" 'How Sexy Are You?' machine. All the little wires are snucked back in place. I would be most honoured if you would do me the pleasure of sticking your little whotsit finger in the hole!"

"No, not this time," I said. "Thanks all the same, Mr Patel, but I've given all that loving stuff up. It makes life too complicated." Mr Patel looked desperately hurt.

"But I have been waiting for you. You must."

"Why?" I asked. "You've got plenty of other customers." Mr Patel mock-punched me on the shoulder.

"Why you? You know why you, you old dog. 'Cause you is the most sexiest boy in the world. If Johnny Casanova uses my machine, all the other little peoples from here and there-abouts will be wanting to do the same thing."

"That's the whole point. Johnny Casanova's dead. I'm just plain Johnny Worms again."

"Trouble with many women, I am guessing?"

"Something like that," I said. "I don't think I'm quite ready for love yet, Mr Patel."

"Balderdash and bunkum," he said. "You is just needing confidence in yourself, Johnny, that is all."

"I don't think so."

"But I do and I know how you can find it."
He was dead clever, Mr Patel. He knew
exactly how to change your mind, just when
you thought you'd made it up.

"A go on the 'How Sexy Are You?' machine?"
I guessed.

"Precisely. Johnny Casanova lives! Please to
hurry, if we are to beat the rush!"

Mr Patel stood proudly by his renovated
machine. Above the painted lady in a bikini
was a sign that he had carefully drawn in
anticipation of my arrival. It said: ARE YOU
AS SEXY AS JOHNNY CASANOVA? 50p
SAYS YOU ARE NOT!

"It's gone up," I observed. "It was only 40p
before."

"It has been mended," said Mr Patel, defensively. "Oh yes, I am imagining great things
for this machine. Do you not think it is a most
attractive sign?"

"It's cool," I admitted, catching sight of my
ruffled hair in the shop window. "Have you
got a comb?" Mr Patel squealed with glee.

"You see, it is working already! And what
is more, for doing this most splendid thing for
me and my family, I give you free goes all
round on the 'How Sexy Are You?' machine
and the clucking chicken."

"Thanks, but no thanks." I shuddered.

177

"The last egg I got out of there caused me one or two problems."

"But I insist," insisted Mr Patel, slipping a coin into the machine and waiting for the chicken to lay an egg. "There, a beautiful, almost real, sparkly necklace. Ideal for parties. Much fun to be had by all who wear her, yes?"

"It's lovely," I replied, accepting Mr Patel's gift reluctantly. "Thanks very much. Shall we get on with the sexy test, only I've got to get home to do my Scripture homework."

"Yes indeed, Mr Johnny, sir. A belief in God is a wonderful thing to sustain you through life, but you are only sexy once, so let's get cracking!" Then, with great ceremony, Mr Patel removed my jacket, rolled up the sleeve of my shirt and placed my index finger into the metal loop on top of the machine. "Be saying cheese!" he shouted, whipping an instant camera out of his overalls and snapping a couple of photos of me in position. "For the publicity for the newspapers," he explained. "And now, it's turn on time!" And he bent down and switched on the "How Sexy Are You?" machine.

At first, everything went perfectly. The machine hummed like a Rolls Royce engine, the lights flashed and my reading slowly rose through TRY PUTTING A PAPER BAG OVER YOUR HEAD and SEXYISH, until it reached LATIN LOVER.

"It's working all right then!" I roared, boorishly, as the machine flashed SNAKE HIPS at me. "I mean, it knows the real McCoy when it sees it!"

"Ha, ha, ha," chuckled Mr Patel. "It is a wondrous sight that is bringing tears of joy to my eyes!" Unfortunately, when the machine hit RED HOT SEX POT Mr Patel's tears of joy turned swiftly to sorrow. Screws loosened, bolts burst and metal panels sprang open as the vibrating machine spilled its gutful of electrical wiring all over the pavement.

"Oh dear," panicked an alarmed Mr Patel. The machine was thrashing around like a beached shark, with my finger trapped in its jaws.

"I think I've broken something!" I screamed.

"Oh, please, not again, no!" Mr Patel wailed, stuffing his handkerchief into his mouth.

"I'm talking about my finger," I yelled. But the machine had burst into flames and Mr Patel was too busy with his fire extinguisher to help me – squirting fountains of foam over his bikinied lovely whose painted body was dripping away between the cracks in the pavement.

When the earth stopped moving and the machine released my finger, I flopped to the ground with a gormless grin stapled to my face like a large, red slice of watermelon.

"Oh dear, oh dear," declared the shattered shopkeeper, weeping over the smoking ruins, "what a bloody turn-up for the books!" Then he helped me to my feet, re-seated me on my bike and shuffled back inside his shop to consume his second bag of jelly babies in as many days. As for me, I rode off in no particular direction, fizzing with ginger and pep and rather pleased with the fact that I was still, and always would be, Johnny Casanova, the unstoppable sex machine.

Floating along on this wave of self-admiration, I absent-mindedly turned into Nelson's Way and came face to face with my Purple Goddess. The sight of her blonde pigtails and bubble gum-munching mouth sent my heart into a spin. She was cycling towards me in her Girl Guide's uniform, which perfectly matched her beautiful blue eyes. She looked good enough to eat. I licked my lips suggestively, and steeled myself for our long overdue meeting. For too long I had kept my feelings secret from this bicycle belle, but today was going to be different. No more Mr Wimp. Hello, Mr Macho! I was in the mood for love. I ran through my flawless plan one more time, just to make sure I hadn't forgotten anything. Bicycle crash, pathetic groaning, tender first aid, then a sweet, mind-blowing, knee-trembling, tonsil-

tickling kiss. Simple. She was close now, wob-
bling slightly to avoid that pothole. I took my
hand out of my pocket (I'd been trying to look
dead hard by riding one-handed) and waved in
her direction. Obviously, she was playing hard
to get, because she didn't respond. I waved
again and this time accompanied it with a
grunted greeting that was meant to sound
butch, but came out sounding vaguely vulgar.

"Heugh!" it went, and she looked up. Oh,
my God, she was looking at me. Those bewil-
dering eyes pierced my heart! This was it. The
moment to crash and die. Now, Johnny, now!
But I couldn't remember what the plan was.
Yes, I could… No, I couldn't! She was getting
away. Then, suddenly, I realized Mr Patel's
necklace was dangling off my middle finger.
I'd pulled it out of my pocket when I waved.
It had to be a sign.

"I say," I yelled, as she sailed past my right
shoulder. "Fancy a necklace?" And she looked
again, only this time there was something to
look at. My bike hit a bump in the road and
knocked the necklace out of my hand. It fell
into the spokes of my front wheel and
wrapped itself round the spindle, stopping the
wheel dead in its tracks. Quite by accident, I
was now having the accident I'd been schem-
ing for and, even better, the object of my desire
was watching. I wanted to make it the best
accident she was ever likely to see, but I'd

181

lost control. I went soaring over the handle-bars like a human cannonball and rolled over on the pavement like a curled-up hedgehog, until my head met a lamppost. There was a sharp crack followed by me screaming. "Owwwww!" I went, and "Aaagggghhh!" Only I wasn't faking. It really had hurt. I really did need her help, but she didn't seem to be interested. Well, come on, I thought, I might be dying for all you know. What was I talking about? I *was* dying! "Help! Little purple vision, help!" But she wasn't looking at me anymore. Call herself a Girl Guide? I thought they were supposed to assist people in distress. She just legged it round the corner. No comforting words, no soothing of my brow, no tender lips pressed sweetly against mine. Nothing! My plan had been a miserable failure. Two weeks in the making, five seconds in the execution and a lifetime of regrets.

"Oh, well," I mused, "things could be worse. At least I haven't broken my leg."

Twenty minutes later, I was on the way to hospital in the back of an ambulance with my leg in a splint. A pair of laughing green eyes stared down at me.

"Hello," I said, "I'm Johnny Casanova. What's a beautiful, green-eyed girl like you doing in an ambulance like this?"

"Looking after you," replied the Irish nurse.

"Do you want to go out with me?" I asked.

"No, thanks," she declined.

"But I'm hot to trot. I'm a red hot chilli pepper with cayenne sauce. I'm a townie tiger with a rrrrrapacious appetite. I'm the unstoppable sex machine!"

"Oh, really," smiled the nurse, "then this won't have any effect on you, will it?" And she shoved a huge great needle full of sleeping stuff into my bum, which knocked my passion on the head faster than a bucket of cold water.

ON BREAKING MY LEG

Ow! It hurts like billio!
It gives me not a thrillio.
But lying here,
Of this I'm clear,
I'm glad it's not my willio!

(Johnny Casanova — floating on gas and air in the back of an ambulance, man)

17

GINGER'S REVENGE

When I came round, my leg felt like a tug-of-war team was pulling it clean out of my hip socket. I screamed just to let everyone know I was still alive and five pairs of eyes appeared in front of me. There were Mum, Dad, Sherene, Nan and Ginger.

"All right, pumpkin?" That was Mum. "You've just broken your leg a little bit, that's all."

"I know that," I said. "Why does it hurt so much?"

"Pongo, get down!" shouted Dad.

" 'Cause Pongo's lying on it, pumpkin," said Mum. Pongo must have done as he was told, because the weight on my leg lifted.

"There," trilled Nan. "All better now, Mr Big Brave Soldier. The dog's gone." And she sat down on the spot which Pongo had just vacated.

"Aaaaaagggggghhhh!"

"Big baby," said Sherene. "I wouldn't cwy if I'd bwoken my leg." The family swirled around in front of my eyes. The pain was first white, then red and then almost bearable.

"Just want you to know," said Mum, "that your dad and I have had a little chat and it's all pumpkin pie again, isn't it, Terry?"

"It is, Babs," said Dad, taking his nose out of *Gnomes and Gardens* for a second. "Your mother and I just want you to know that we love you, Johnny."

"Keep your voice down, will you?" I hissed.

"And I love you too," chipped in Sherene, flinging her arms around my neck. "Vewy, vewy, vewy much, ath it happenth."

"Yeah, all right!" I said, pushing her off.

"Actually, I don't," she added. "I jutht thaid that 'cauthe Mummy told me to."

"Yeah, and it's lovely to see you lot, as well." I forced a smile. "I think I'll get some sleep now, if you don't mind."

"Oh no, you can't go to sleep," said Mum. "We've got a lovely little surprise for you, haven't we, Ginger?"

"Yeah," replied my best mate.

"Hello, Ginger," I said.

"Hello, Johnny."

"Are we best friends again?"

"Yeah," he said. "I've brought a few people in to cheer you up!"

185

"I hope they're not girls."

"Why?" he asked.

"Well, I wouldn't want them to see me looking like this, would I?" Ginger looked at my mum, like he was saying "I didn't think he knew", and then turned back to me.

"Looking like what?" he said, cautiously.

"In my pyjamas," I replied. "And I haven't done my hair, have I? How does it look?"

"Oh, your hair," faltered Ginger. "Your hair looks … smooth," he said.

"Well, go on then, wheel 'em in, these surprise visitors." And off he went, with Mum and Dad patting him on the back like he was part of the family and Sherene making moony eyes behind his back.

"Johnny," said Mum, once Ginger had left the ward. "I think there's something you should know, before you see your visitors. It's about your head, pumpkin…" Something was up. Nobody would look me in the eye, not even Pongo.

"What about my head?" I asked, cagily.

"You got a few bumps and scratches, pumpkin, when you fell off your bike."

"Could I have a mirror, please?" I said, sensing that something was amiss. I could hear Ginger coming down the corridor with my visitors. They were giggling. That meant they were girls!

"I don't think you should look in a mirror,

actually, Johnny," said Mum. "Not now. It'll only upset you." Upset me? What had they done?

"I haven't had brain surgery, have I?" I panicked, sitting up in bed and stretching my broken leg. "Aaaaggghhh!"

"No, it's much worse than that, pumpkin."

"Worse than brain surgery!" My mouth had gone dry. She was going to tell me I only had three weeks to live!

"You've had four stitches in your scalp."

"YES," I bellowed, "AND?" The suspense would kill me if the brain damage didn't.

"And they had to ... you know ... do what they always do."

"WHICH IS WHAT?" I bawled.

"Shave your hair off!" said Mum. I put my hands on top of my head to confirm the dreadful news and touched skin.

"GET ME A MIRROR NOW!" I cried, just as the door to the ward swung open and Ginger came in with my visitors.

"I thought you'd be pleased to see them," Ginger said, suppressing a sly snigger.

"Hello, Johnny," simpered Alison Mallinson.

"Ginger told us about the crash," smiled Mia Theopopilopolus.

"And I just wanted to say how sorry I am," added the Purple Goddess.

"So where's your hair then?" slurped Deborah Smeeton. "Why does your head look like a

187

bottom?" At which point Ginger exploded into helpless giggles at the foot of my bed, while Sherene passed me a mirror, which confirmed that I was indeed as bald as a bed post. I tried to stay calm. I tried to keep smiling like none of it mattered, like it was of no consequence to me that the three most delectable women I'd ever met were seeing me bald and in PJs, but the embarrassment was just too enormous, too life-shattering to bear, and it wasn't helped by Ginger's childish tittering.

"Johnny, look," he roared. "Look, O Sacred Hairless One, outside the window. Flying pigs!" Ginger's revenge was sweet. Slowly, with what little dignity I could muster, I edged down my bed and pulled the sheet up over my head.

"Johnny Casanova?" called a voice that I didn't recognize. "Flowers for Johnny Casanova."

"Over here," I whispered.

"Flowers from Mr Patel," said the nurse. "To Johnny Casanova, the unstoppable sex machine."

I groaned.

I squirmed.

I wanted to die.

Then I rang the bell by the side of my bed for a doctor to come and advise me on the quickest way to do it.

ROMEO'S RETURN

I'll be back,
The girls demand it.
I'll be back,
To play luv's fool.
I'll be back,
As J. Casanova.
All I need's
A wig for school.

(Johnny Casanova, Aged 13 — From his
most recent collection of poems, 'Luv
Wears Big Boots With Steel Toe Caps')